Velvet Door Society

Shanaya Fastje

2016, TWB Press

www.twbpress.com

Prologue
Soul Thief

Standing under the canopy of a closed business entrance, he watched derelicts drink alcohol outside a grubby nightclub, one of only two in Rosaphene, Virginia. They hollered and scuffled among themselves. The smell of cigarette smoke disturbed his nostrils and stirred a sense of impatience. Electronic dance music rumbled across the usually quiet street, and his annoyance grew stronger with the intense vibration of the heavy bass. Observing humanity's fragility and idiocy always entertained him. He felt nobler than the fools who considered wolf whistles and yelling crude comments at passing women a form of flattery.

Near closing time, as inebriated and exhausted patrons poured out of the nightclub, he scanned the crowd carefully, waiting to see her, waiting to feel her energy. A flickering streetlight annoyed him further, so he strode across the street in anticipation of seeing her, unable to wait for her at a distance any longer.

Dodging trash thrown carelessly on the ground, he reached the sidewalk in time to see her amble out of the club with her head held high. His heart skipped a beat. Her silky blonde hair bounced with every step she took, but he wasn't here to admire her.

He was here to take her life.

He slinked into the dark alleyway beside the club, pressed his back against the cold brick wall, and heard the squeaks of rodents foraging for food in an overflowing dumpster. The smell of garbage and urine almost made him rethink his point of attack. Almost.

While humming an obscure melody, she walked in his direction, probably toward her apartment.

He scowled. *Little did she know she would never make it home.*

As she passed the dark alley's maw, he lunged forward, covered her mouth with his gloved hand, and wrestled her deeper into the shadows.

Her screams muffled, inaudible behind the continuous thumping music, she managed only guttural cries, kicked and squirmed. Oh how he delighted in her desperation. He shoved her thin frame against the wall and pressed his body against hers as her eyes darted back and forth rapidly, her eyelashes fluttering with fear.

"Don't be afraid," he rasped into her ear, his excited breath heavy against her skin. "This will be quick, but I can't promise painless."

She stopped fighting. Her eyes bore into his face with terrified recognition.

"That's better." He removed his hand from her mouth and stepped back.

She gritted her teeth. "It's *you*."

With a smirk, he wrapped his fingers around the garnet stone hanging from a chain around her neck. "You should have known it would come to this." He yanked her necklace hard enough to break the chain.

The force caused her head to snap back. "Why *me*?"

He clutched the stone in his fist. "My plans for humanity have just begun, but first, I must rid this world of your kind."

"Please." Her body shuddered. "We only want to exist in peace."

He clamped the oddly shaped stone between his teeth, freeing his hands.

"Are you going to kill me...like the others?"

He reached into the left pocket of his black trench coat and pulled out a syringe.

"What's that for?"

From his other pocket, he retrieved a gold lighter, clicked open the lid, and flicked the wick into flame.

Her eyes widened. "No. Please no."

He tossed the lighter at her. The small flame instantly ignited her body into a blazing inferno, bright and excruciatingly hot.

Engulfed in fire, she screamed, but the infernal music drowned out the last sound she made on earth.

Basking in the warmth, he watched the young woman's body dissolve into a pile of ash where she once stood. Then a cloud of purple light rose up from the ashes and illuminated the alleyway with its vividness.

The brilliant display never ceased to amaze him, the energy of the spirit's soul profound and unseen by human eyes. He stepped forward with the syringe and sucked in all the purple light, which made the cylinder glow. Wasting no time, he slid the left coat sleeve up his arm and stabbed the needle into a throbbing, expectant vein in his wrist. Excitement caused his right hand to tremble as he pressed the plunger full in, not slowly, but with one smooth stroke.

Darkness reclaimed the alleyway.

Throwing his head back in bliss, he bit down

on the stone and savored the heat and energy glowing within his chest. He freed his mind and felt nothing but exuberance and jubilation. Even the annoying music faded from his consciousness. He felt no guilt, no regret, no sorrow for the soul he'd just stolen. He'd need that energy and more to see his plans for this world come to fruition.

With the syringe safely back in his pocket, he released the garnet stone from his teeth and dropped it into the pile of ash. The authorities would find it: evidence of his success, a means to identify the ashes, and a sure way to instill fear throughout the spirit community.

He stooped to retrieve his special gold lighter from the ground and spoke his final words to the ashes. "Your friends are next."

Chapter 1
STRANGERS AND CROWS

When we look up at the stars, we are not watching the sky... the sky is watching us.

Willow remembered her father warning her to be careful when talking to the stars, to never tell them something she wouldn't tell her best friend. Stars were gossipers. Loud mouths. As soon as the sun rose and they were seen no more, they would laugh and share stories with each other about the poor saps with their materialistic, unattainable, selfish little wishes.

As she grew older, she would often question her father. "But stars can't talk."

Her father would smirk and lean in close to her. "That's what they want you to think," he would whisper.

The idea of stars having very human-like qualities sparked Willow to become wildly interested in all things astrological. Of course, only she considered herself to be wildly interested; everyone else considered her wildly obsessed. She grew out of her obsessive interest, but it still lingered, and she still had an appreciation for the stars.

Willow was in a reverie and didn't remember drawing the constellation Leo on the top of her left hand with a blue ballpoint pen she had found on the table in her mother's psychiatrist's dimly lit and slightly cold waiting room, which looked more like a vampire's living room with its black velvet chairs and dark red walls. It wasn't the most calming or pleasant place. In her head, the office was haunted with ghosts occupying the space around her: floating, staring, or even *smelling.* She shivered at the thought of a rude and invasive ghost sniffing her. Willow often thought weird things to keep from going crazy with boredom.

The old grandfather clock in one corner struck two o'clock. She wondered why her mother took so long talking to Dr. Everly. *Probably gossiping. Like the stars.*

The entrance door creaked open and in walked a tall, pale dark-haired young man who looked overly confident, with a smirk on his face and a sway in his step. He plopped on the seat next to Willow, and naturally, she avoided any conversation with him. Fighting nervousness, she started to draw another constellation on her right hand. Whenever she engaged in human interaction, the result was almost always embarrassment. She didn't *like* to start trouble, but she couldn't help but find joy in getting a rise out of people she didn't particularly like.

"Pisces," he said as he curiously examined her hand. "Are you a Pisces?"

Willow just nodded, playing the shy card. *Please stop talking,* she repeated over and over in her head. She toyed with the ruby ring on her right ring finger and tried her best to tune him out.

"Twelfth sign. Represented by a pair of fish. Am I wrong?" he asked.

She could tell that he loved the sound of his own voice and wondered if bothering girls was a hobby of his, but it would be rude of her to ignore him. "Dead on," she mumbled.

"Ruled by Jupiter and Neptune. Let me guess...you were born in February." He was no longer looking at her hand but at the side of her face.

February 20th, she answered in her head. As much as she hated to think about it, she was a little bit impressed—but just a little bit. Mostly because she didn't know other people who were interested or even mildly educated on zodiac signs. "How'd you guess February?" she asked and finally turned to look at him. Since her plan to avoid conversation failed, she came up with a new plan. No *eye* contact. Looking at his jaw line, she saw that he had flawless skin.

"Was I right?"

He seemed like a person who was often unsatisfied with rejection. Before she answered, she had to take a moment to squirm in her seat due to physical and mental discomfort. "February 20th." Immediately, she regretted her decision to respond. She shifted her attention to the floor.

As if on cue, the door to Dr. Eira Everly's office finally opened. Out walked the skinny, darkly dressed doctor with Willow's mother, Elizabeth Ferring. Willow took a deep breath and thanked the gods up above for the interruption.

"Evander, I wasn't expecting you until three," Dr. Everly exclaimed in the young man's direction, completely ignoring Willow.

He stood and hugged Dr. Everly gently and spoke inaudibly into her shoulder.

Willow couldn't help but watch the doctor and that strange young man hugging. It was like watching the scene of a car crash on the side of the road; she simply couldn't look away. Dr. Everly seemed cold to him, which sent chills down Willow's spine. The image of the doctor having any interaction with another person besides a simple handshake felt odd. However, she and Evander parted soon enough, and the world was once again balanced—as balanced as this world could possibly get.

"I'll see you next time," Dr. Everly said to Elizabeth. The doctor seldom let silence come between anyone; words always had to be spoken, stories always had to be told, so she continued to make small talk with Elizabeth. Meanwhile, Evander gave Willow strange vibes, but she didn't know if they were more good than bad. She didn't want to find out and decided to skitter out of that tiny room as fast as possible.

"Where are your manners, Willow?" Her mother spoke in a threatening tone. "Aren't you going to say goodbye to your friend?"

She must've thought everyone Willow talked to was her friend.

Willow slumped to Evander and held out her left hand for him to take, which was a pretty big move for her, considering her qualms for making physical contact with guys she didn't know. "Very nice meeting you." She accidentally made eye contact. A jolt of trepidation shot through her chest. She gulped as he slowly took her hand and leaned in to kiss it as if they were characters in an old Shakespearian play.

"It was very nice meeting you too, Willow." The way he said her name almost made her topple backwards. He had the perfect look and personality to be a serial killer. She scolded herself for completely stereotyping someone she didn't know.

Evander stared at the top of the hand he'd kissed, and then looked up and squinted at her. "Fifth sign. Ruled by the sun and represented by a lion."

Willow nodded quickly.

Evander let out a tiny laugh.

"What's funny?" she demanded.

"I'm a Leo." He showed her a smirk. "I hope our paths will cross again one day."

***

Willow remained quiet during the ride back to her house. It started to rain. She leaned her head against the cold glass window. In Rosaphene, Virginia, it rained on occasion, snowed heavily during the winter, and became annoyingly hot during the summer. It was fall, and the October weather was every kind of perfect. Thunder and rain were lullabies for Willow. She also loved lightning way more than fireworks.

The sound of the rain hitting the top of the car and the thunder rumbling the earth kept her awake. She thought about Evander's eyes. Though she couldn't have looked at them for more than a few seconds, the image was crystal clear in the back of her head. She wasn't the type of person to notice every little feature of a person. Eyes were eyes, hair was hair, and lips were lips. People were people. But there was something about his eyes that stoked her curiosity.

A sudden feeling of discomfort overwhelmed her.

She couldn't find the words to describe Evander's eyes.

Home now, Willow sleepily walked behind her mother into their house and headed straight to the kitchen. She wasn't happy to be home and wished there were errands to run or business to attend to just so that she could spend more time away from that *house*.

The soles of their shoes, wet from the rain, squeaked on the hardwood floor. Willow pulled out a box of waffles from the freezer and popped a waffle into the toaster while she ate one frozen.

Her mother leaned over their marble kitchen island and eyed her while she chewed and swallowed.

"How are you feeling?"

"A little hungry. How are you feeling?" Willow took another bite. Chewed. Swallowed.

"I told Dr. Everly that you seemed distant lately, and she agreed."

"She thinks I'm distant even when I'm not." Another bite. Chewed. Swallowed.

"You should consider talking to her."

"I don't trust her."

"You need to trust her."

"That's the thing," another bite, "I don't need to do anything," chewed, "and I won't trust her," swallowed. "She acts like she's a thousand years old and knows everything."

Elizabeth stomped over to Willow, grabbed the waffle out of her hand, and threw it in the trash at the exact moment the waffle in the toaster popped out.

Willow grabbed it and took a bite, burning her tongue.

Her mother clenched her jaw. "You should talk to her about your little...*dreams*."

"Can I please eat my carbs in peace?"

"Why do you have to be so stubborn?"

"I won't tell her about my dreams. I wouldn't have told you about them if I knew you were going to keep pushing me to talk about them...as if they're terrible burdens on the family." Willow channeled her inner anger and walked past her mother to the spiral staircase leading upstairs to her bedroom.

She kicked out of her worn leather boots and lounged on her window seat. Outside her window stood a big mulberry tree. Birds nested in it, and she had a perfect view of them. She was pretty sure they were Robins, judging by their color. Just the word *color* made her think about Evander's eyes again. She created a list in her head of all the things she knew were blue, and then drifted off into another daze.

Willow was naturally shy and reserved, but after what happened during her last year of school, she became quieter than usual, mostly because she was thinking, and when she thought, she got quiet. When she, or anyone for that matter, became quiet, people tended to worry. She thought about fate and destiny, but also about fictional characters from television shows she had binge-watched. Her mother often worried that Willow was damaged, scared or even angry, and sometimes Willow was all or some of those things.

Most of the time though, she wasn't. She was just thinking.

She attended one of only three high schools in the city. When her school made the front page of the local newspaper, it wasn't because the students had done great community service or won a contest. It was because one of the students had been beaten to death, and two others were hospitalized with serious injuries. Sparing the details of the argument, in the end, ten kids were involved in the same scuffle. When her mother heard about what had happened that day, her paranoia escalated, and Willow had to spend most of her after-school time in the quiet of her own bedroom, and that continued after she graduated.

Willow couldn't decide whether she missed school or not. Though she definitely knew that she did not miss the plastic-tasting cafeteria food, the different colored bubble gum placed purposely all over walls and desks, the crude writing on bathroom stalls, or the weird smell that came from the Janitor's closet near her English class. At first, she thought the odor must have been a skunk. She convinced herself, for two years, that the janitor had a pet skunk, and he was hiding it in the closet. But as time passed, she figured a forest animal making itself comfortable among brooms and cleaning chemicals wasn't the source of the smell; it was marijuana.

Her window rattled. A crow had accidentally flown into it, pulling Willow out of her musing. She jumped up and watched the black bird flap its wings and fly away. *Poor thing.*

Suddenly there was a knock at her door. Her mother's voice creaked through the thick wooden walls, notifying Willow that there was pizza waiting for her downstairs, a snack to hold them over until dinner.

***

"Why did Dr. Everly take forever talking to you today?" Willow asked then stuffed the pointy end of the pepperoni pizza slice into her mouth.

Elizabeth sat cross-legged with Willow on their oversized sofa in the living room and wiped her mouth with a napkin. "I was telling her that you were incredibly bright about the stars and the sky."

The sound of a car's engine roared up in front of their house. Willow and her mother exchanged scared looks. Elizabeth pushed the box of pizza to Willow. "Hide it."

She immediately ran up to her room to hide the pizza under her bed.

Mr. Joel Ferring hated most junk food, including pizza, and forbade it in the house. Her father called it the deep-dish-of-diabetes.

Before she left her room, Willow noticed the black bird sitting on a branch of the tree in front of her window, peering through. She walked to the window and unlatched the locks to open it up. "Are you the bird that crashed into my window?"

The bird sat still on the branch.

She slowly reached her hand to the bird and began to stroke its head with two fingers.

It ruffled its feathers and tipped its beak down, making itself comfortable under Willow's touch. The little crow closed its little crow eyes and made small noises, at which Willow couldn't help but smile.

Her mother yelled from downstairs, beckoning her to dinner. She yelled back that she was on her way, and stroked the bird's head one last time.

***

At the dinner table, her father asked, "How did your appointment go earlier today?"

Elizabeth smiled happily. "Very well. We spoke quite a bit about Willow."

"Dr. Everly thinks I'm distant," Willow said. "Which is funny, because Dr. Everly hardly ever speaks directly to me, spends most of her time with Mom."

He stuffed a forkful of broccoli into his mouth. "Don't let her brainwash you, Elizabeth. And don't let her brainwash our daughter either."

"She's not brainwashing me," Elizabeth exclaimed before Willow could say another word.

He swallowed. "That woman gives me bad vibes, Lizzie."

"Everyone gives you bad vibes, Joel."

"All right," Willow said, wanting to be in any other situation than the one she was in. "I'm fine. We're both fine."

They ignored her.

"Neither of you need a doctor to spew lies and scam us out of our money," Joel bellowed.

"Whatever you say, Joel. You seem to know everything about psychiatry. Maybe *you* should talk to me instead, so we don't get scammed out of our money." Elizabeth grabbed her plate and threw what was left of her food in the trash before heading toward her bedroom down the hall.

Willow's father dropped his fork on his plate, causing a sharp bang to fill the room. He ran his fingers through his hair and leaned back in his chair, grunting out of frustration.

"I think she's fussy because she doesn't want

you to be right," Willow said while picking up her dad's almost-empty plate to put it in the sink along with hers.

"She never wants me to be right." Joel ripped the tie from his neck. Willow heard his dress shoes click down the stairs to the basement, and she was left standing in the middle of her kitchen alone.

Mr. and Mrs. Ferring's marriage was dysfunctional, to say the least. Their personalities were nearly alike: erratic and dramatic. Willow was surprised her own personality wasn't as strong and pessimistic as theirs. But then she remembered that two negatives made a positive. Her family had no balance. It was her mother's way or no way, or her father's way or no way. No negotiations were made and there was no meeting at a middle ground. Willow felt uncomfortable being in the middle of two very immature adults. No wonder she hated this house.

I'm raising my parents.

She grabbed a black flannel coat from the hall closet then knocked three times on her parents' bedroom door.

"What do you want?"

She opened the door a crack. "I'm going to Crossroads."

Her mother moaned. "You better get back here

soon."

"I won't be long."

"Close the door."

Willow nodded and did as she was told.

When she had turned thirteen, her parents allowed her to go down to the Art District about a mile away. The Art District took up five blocks of downtown. It was famous for its vintage shops, mini museums, cafés, and florists. Willow's favorite place was Crossroads, a coffee shop where the baristas knew her name and favorite drink. She'd made good friends with the manager there, Zan. He was only in his twenties but already had a degree in business. Zan could open his own coffee shop if he wanted to, but he was content managing Crossroads. It made him happy, and no one should ever have to stop doing what made them happy.

She developed a fondness for other regular customers of Crossroads. One person in particular was a man named Clarence whom she would say was one of her favorite people. She found Clarence difficult to describe because of his eccentricity and distance from normalcy. He had a knack for breaking laws he thought were stupid; he listened to classic rock; and once he wore a suit made entirely of cheese slices. Clarence was a little more than double Willow's age, but she felt like she had a better friendship with him than she had with most people younger than forty. Willow learned a lot from him because he seemed so wise and confident in his opinions of humanity. As she walked down her street, she hoped she would see him at Crossroads.

The sidewalk was wet from the rain. There was still a light drizzle, but Willow didn't mind the dampness. She trotted down the hill from where they lived. Forests and mountains surrounded the quiet city of Rosaphene; it was eerie, especially when it rained. But when it was summertime, the always-shining sun hit the buildings and trees beautifully. The city looked different every season and grew lovelier each year, like it constantly shed its old skin and grew into a new one.

It only took Willow ten minutes to get downtown. She opened the door to Crossroads and scanned the room. Clarence was sitting at at table with a newspaper in his hands. He'd dressed in pale pink pants, a blue button down shirt, and a light brown suede blazer. She wondered if he even *owned* a mirror.

So as not to disturb his reading, she slipped by him and rang the little silver bell on the unattended counter.

Zan rushed out from the back, carrying a crate full of assorted coffee bean packets. He smiled at her and carefully placed the box on the floor. There were usually one or two people working the evening shift. Usually it was Zan because he liked working late. Both he and Willow appreciated the night, which was just one of the many things they had in common.

"The usual?" Zan grabbed a large cup before she could confirm his assumption. *The usual* was a large cinnamon latte with a shot of caramel, vanilla syrup, and extra whipped cream with nutmeg sprinkled on top. That particular order provided her with the exact amount of caffeine she needed. Trying to survive without good coffee would be like trying to survive without oxygen.

Zan whipped up her drink.

Willow slid a five-dollar bill across the counter.

Zan made no effort to take it. "My treat." He smiled.

"Just take the money, Zan."

"What don't you understand about *my treat*?"

Willow laughed and rolled her eyes. "Fine." She stuck the five dollars back in her pocket and jumped up to sit on the counter. She twisted her legs to the other side so she could face Zan.

He leaned his back on the wall across from her

and folded his arms as if waiting for her to rant about her dreams. When she didn't, he must've decided to lead the conversation. "Have any good dreams lately?" Zan looked down at his feet.

She took a sip of her latte. "I haven't been sleeping much."

"Are you scared?"

"Is that what you think?" Willow twisted away from Zan then jumped off the counter.

He hurried out from behind the barista bar and put his hands on Willow's shoulders. "Sorry."

"Or do you think I'm crazy?"

"I never said that." Zan took his hands off her shoulders and patted her cheek. "Bad day, huh?"

She stole a look at Clarence, still reading his paper. "It's my mom again. She wants me to see a shrink."

Ever since Willow was a young child, she had trouble telling the difference between reality and dreams. There were a few steps she would often take in order to quickly recognize whether she was dreaming or awake. She would look at her hand and count her fingers; if there weren't five on each hand, she knew she was in a dream. As she grew older, she learned how to control most aspects of her dreams. She could change settings, dictate outcomes, and even choose people she encountered.

Something she couldn't master was controlling a nightmare. It seemed as though every time she tried, the situation she was in would only worsen. The man chasing her would run faster, the room would get darker, or her eyes grew blinder. A rapid heart rate and cold sweats would often wake her up.

There was so much she wanted to tell him about her dreams but couldn't. When she first told her mother, Elizabeth had a panic attack and asked her to seek help; and she hadn't stopped asking since. Willow knew that Zan was there for her if she ever needed to vent, but she was still scared that he would think there was something seriously wrong with her if she told him too much.

A customer walked into Crossroads, followed by the sound of a ringing bell. Zan returned to his position behind the counter and greeted the tall man whose hat bill shadowed his face.

Willow stepped to the side and sat at a small table by the front window, so she had a view outside and a view of Zan and his customer who ordered a large mint tea.

Clarence looked up from his paper and asked her, "How do you feel about kayaking?"

She giggled, not surprised by Clarence's

random question. "I feel indifferent, much like all water sports."

"It's quite fun. You should try it sometime. Would you like some company?"

She waved her hand at the chair across from her. "Please."

Clarence switched seats, rather ungracefully, tripping over his feet, then sat down and set the newspaper on his lap. "What's all this I hear about dreams?"

"Clarence, were you eavesdropping on our *private conversation*?"

"I wouldn't if you weren't so loud about it."

"There's something I actually wanted to talk to you about."

He folded his hands on the table. "Well, let's have it then."

Willow took a deep breath. She didn't like talking about herself, but she was convinced the best advice she could get would come from Clarence. "When you were my age, did you know what you wanted to do with your life?"

He squinted and gazed outside the window, as if the answer lay somewhere with the setting sun. His dark brown hair was disheveled; wild strands stuck up all over the place.

"I'm just...struggling."

"Every life-struggle is different. I've had the opportunity to travel, see the world, and do many odd jobs, some of which, you know, had landed me in sticky situations, literally and figuratively. Seen a lot of love. Seen a lot of hate. I learnt that what you do and who you know is of less importance than treating everyone with kindness. Goes a long way, you know."

Clarence, forever the philosopher. "But what am I supposed to do from here? Go to college? Find a job somewhere and save up for my retirement? How boring is all that?"

"Number one, take pride in what you're passionate about, and number two, stop worrying so much about where you'll be thirty years from now. Enjoy today. It's the only one you're going to get."

"You make life sound so easy."

"It's up to you to make your life exciting. Find ways to make boring days fun."

"You mean like you, getting arrested."

"Shhh." He shook his head but continued to smile. "Try not to do anything illegal. Learn from my mistakes."

"In your defense, I don't think you realized that what you were doing was illegal."

"Enough about me." He huffed. "Be

spontaneous, Willow. Do good. I do believe that destiny tends to inspire us when we get lost in life. Before you know it, you'll be in the exact position you never dreamed you wanted to be in."

"I'm not easily inspired."

Clarence closed one eye and tilted his head to the side. She never grew tired of watching him mix strange facial expressions. "Inspiration is everywhere." He retrieved the newspaper from his lap and set it on the table. "Find inspiration in here."

She looked at him with a skeptical slant to her brow, confused about how she'd find inspiration from the newspaper. Nothing eventful ever happened in Rosaphene; it just wasn't an exciting town.

Clarence stood. "Trust me." He strolled out, not a care in the world. His receding form disappeared in the glare of the front window like a fading mirage, or like he'd vanished into thin air.

She heard the customer say, "Keep the change," as he slapped money down on the counter, and then he headed toward the front door. When his hand met the door, he froze and slowly turned to look straight at her. "What a weird coincidence."

Now she recognized his voice but wished she

hadn't. She shifted her gaze to see Evander as he approached her table.

"Willow, right?" He stuck out his hand for her to take.

She eyed his slender fingers, recalled his dramatic gallantness earlier, and declined a repeat performance. "Evander," she muttered, annoyed.

"Fancy meeting you here." He offered a smile and sat on the chair across from her without asking for permission.

She would have been much happier if he had just left her alone. She could've sworn his hair was lighter, but shockingly, tonight it was jet black. His face had the same pale complexion. His eyes were the same mesmerizing blue.

"This *is* weird." She swished the coffee around in her cup. "I didn't expect to see you again, especially not today."

Evander smirked. "Would you find it strange if I said I *knew* I'd see you again?"

"You're forgetting one thing. I don't talk to strangers." Willow swallowed hard.

"All friends were strangers once."

Her nerves were peaking. She thought she'd start shaking uncontrollably and possibly have a mini seizure. Evander hadn't gotten the chance to say much, but Willow heard his words shoot out of his mouth faster than a bullet from a gun. She took a deep breath and focused on her latte. "I don't...I...look, I don't want to be rude, but whatever game this is...or whoever paid you to harass me—"

Before she could finish her sentence, the window next to her rattled. A black crow had flown directly into the glass. Fighting panic, she held her hand against her rapidly beating heart, her eyes wide open in shock and a touch of déjà vu.

The bird flew away.

Evander squinted at her. "You've seen that bird before, haven't you?"

Willow couldn't calm her palpitating heart.

"Either that or you've just seen a ghost." Evander sat forward on the edge of his seat. "Which is it?"

She knew it was the same crow that had flown into her bedroom window, though she didn't understand how easily she recognized a particular crow when they all looked alike. Evander's odd reaction may have been the root of why she was overreacting to the incident. It could have just been a coincidence. After all, weirder things had happened to her. Then she wondered if Evander was some kind of psychic. *He's not a psychic,*

Willow argued with herself. *This is ridiculous. He's just a creepy stalker.*

"Have you been following me...like that bird?" Willow shifted her body and ignored her thumping heartbeat.

"So you *have* seen that bird before."

"What's it to you?"

He leaned back in his chair and gazed out the window. "I didn't follow you here, but that bird obviously did."

Willow gripped her cup, wondering if the coffee was hot enough to use as a weapon against Evander if he attacked her. "Please, leave me alone."

"Let me show you something first."

"What?" She stood and he stood with her, towering eight inches over her, which would've been intimidating if Willow was easily intimidated by height.

"After I show you, if you still want me to leave you alone, I will. But I won't unless you see what I want you to see."

"What do you want to show me?" Willow tossed her cup into the trash behind Evander and crossed her arms.

"I can't tell you."

"You can only show me?"

"You're a quick learner." He set down his coffee, produced a pen from his pocket, and then gently picked up Willow's wrist. "Meet me here tomorrow, around this same time." He scribbled an address on her hand.

"You don't plan to murder me and sell my organs, right?"

"No murder will take place, though I'm sure a murderer would say the same thing. Do me a favor and *actually* show up." He picked up his cup and backed out of the coffee shop. "Don't stand me up."

From the backroom doorway, Zan peered at a shell-shocked Willow. "What the hell was that all about?"

She said nothing in response, didn't move from where she stood either. Instead, she stared out the window, fighting an urge to flee home.

"Sounds like you have a date." Zan wiped his hands on a towel. "Where did you meet *him*?"

"At Dr. Everly's office today."

"Was it love at first sight?" Zan joked.

Willow groaned. She wasn't a romantic, not in the least. She was never one for chick flicks, planning a wedding she didn't know she would ever have, or hoping a secret admirer would leave a dozen roses on her doorstep on Valentine's Day.

She didn't think she would ever love someone.

Love was some kind of monster in her closet, taunting her to take a peek, but fear kept her from looking. She'd wrap herself in her blanket at night, listen to the growling in her closet, and shut her eyes tight. Love meant attraction and infatuation, and all things pink and red. However, love was risk and vulnerability. And especially, for her, love was paranoia. She had her parents to thank for that. She thought if she ever did fall in love, she would fall *too* much in love, and her heart would explode into billions of pieces.

She'd heard people say that one could never care *too* much about someone, but she strongly disagreed. So love was something she had steered clear of. She'd sworn she always would, but that was before she figured out that love was not a one-size-fits-all phenomena, and everyone loved in different ways. But love at first sight? Not even close.

She tried to think of any reason why Evander would run into her only hours after she had met him at—of all places to meet someone—her mother's psychiatrist's office. Perhaps because Rosaphene was a small town, tonight really was just a coincidence. Or Evander was totally following her, and there was some kind of conspiracy going on between him and that stupid crow.

She didn't like Evander. He was full of himself. She could never fall for someone like him. However, her curiosity about him was stronger than her fear. Common sense told her not to meet him at some random address late in the afternoon tomorrow, but Clarence had told her to make her life exciting. Besides, she actually wanted to see what Evander had to show her.

She looked down at the newspaper on the table. The headline read: *Another Mysterious Murder in Rosaphene*. Her heart lurched. Was finding the murderer the inspiration Clarence was talking about?

***

Hot anger flooded Zan's chest. He ached to help Willow, to warn her about meeting with someone she knew nothing about. The thought of Willow getting herself into some of the same disasters he had gotten himself into many times before, made him want to protect her from the hurt that Evander caused.

Zan knew that he wouldn't be able to control her or change her mind when she was set on a decision, but he still wanted to try his best to support her and guide her in all the right ways, even though guiding her wasn't his job. Being taken advantage of was an awful feeling that was hard to shake. After Evander had deceived him, it took Zan a while to realize that not everyone was out to get him, but he was still wary of people's intentions.

Life in Rosaphene was supposed to be lackluster. It was a small town where everyone knew each other's name. For once, Zan actually felt at peace. He had surrounded himself with good people, and he wasn't going to let Evander take anything good away from him again.

***

Willow said her goodbyes to Zan and took her sweet time walking home, taking time to breathe in the clean air with long, deep breaths. She watched the sky go from grey to slate. The trees she passed under dripped cold-water droplets on her head, sending chills down her arms from the sting of the cold.

Willow was an expert at dosing off. She mastered the talent of walking steadily while her mind ran quickly into a world that had no end. Some people thought a human brain was like a computer or machine, but to Willow, it was more like having a universe in her skull, a galaxy, a Milky Way of thoughts and ideas, some scary and some so exciting that real life was boring. In her head, no one questioned her or put a label on her because of a simple human characteristic. *Dreamer*.

She wished other people would understand that she didn't cast a shadow over reality because she didn't like living or because she was bitter toward the world. She lived in her dreams because they were fun, knowledgeable, and enchanting. There were things this world lacked sometimes, but they were things she craved and never stopped craving.

When she reached the porch of her two-story brick house that needed new shingles, she sighed. She knew exactly why she hated coming home to that house. The energy changed every time she walked inside, she could feel it. It was thick and dark. All was fairly good in the world around her, except for what went on in that house: the tension, the bickering, and the fighting. She hadn't lived here all her life. She and her family moved in when she was ten. She never liked its personality, compared it to a storybook villain, but she just couldn't convince her parents to find a kinder place to call home.

With trepidation gnawing at her ribs, she

turned the front door knob. It was unlocked, just as she had left it. The house was dark and quiet, also just as she had left it. She climbed the stairs to her bedroom, threw her coat on the floor and flopped on her bed. The room smelled like pizza, reminding her of where she stashed it. She rolled over, reached under the bed, and slid the box out.

Chewing pizza, she lay back and looked up at the little glow-in-the-dark stars she had stuck to her ceiling years before. She loved the stars, regardless of all the fables her father used to tell her about them being gossipers. Stars were the epitome of happiness and hope. They were on top of the world, literally.

She'd read many popular phrases about guiding lights and dark tunnels, and she trusted many of those phrases. Life wasn't all about rainbows and butterflies. It wasn't supposed to be perfect. If life were perfect, no one would grow and no one would learn from their mistakes. If everyone was happy every minute of the day and every day of the year, everyone would be smiling clones, living meaninglessly. The turmoil and what people did with it, how they overcame adversity, and how they helped other people, those things made life meaningful. When she looked at the stars, she remembered that she was never alone, as long as she had the stars to talk to her.

She finished her pizza, fell asleep, and dreamed a dream.

***

Willow found herself standing in a large, dimly lit room with one floor lamp in the far left corner. The walls were painted black, and some of the paint had chipped off. There was one battered door—the door she'd stepped through to enter the room—along with eight windows, two on every wall. The glass shielded her from a rainstorm outside.

In the center of the room sat a beautiful piano that looked as if it needed a good dusting. She immediately walked to one of the windows, the floorboards squeaked under her feet, and looked outside, taking notice that she was on a beach. The ocean waves slammed against giant rocks, and thunder rumbled from big grey clouds, and barely peeking through, the sun sent down its beams of light on the wild water.

She spun around, sat on the piano bench, and traced her cold fingers on the keys. Exquisite notes echoed through the room, producing clear, crisp sound. She looked at her hands, counted her fingers just to make sure she was dreaming, noticed she had only three on each hand, and put them both down to resume playing. She didn't know how to play piano, but she played like she had known how for years. She held one last chord then rose from the bench and walked up to the beat-up door. The doorknob was a fancy crystal knob that hurt her hand when she turned it.

As she visualized the beach on a clear day, violent winds almost knocked her down. She looked up to the sky and sighed heavily, about to scold the weather, when the rain stopped and the clouds moved away quickly, finally releasing the full power of the sun that was once hiding.

***

Willow woke up the next morning with the sunrise. She moaned into her pillow, as she loathed waking up in the morning, struggled with her love to be awake early, but she hated to actually get up early. The sun, she imagined, mocked her. Its rays grew harsher by the second, as if yelling at her to get out of bed. The sun was a bully, tormenting her with its light. She lazily climbed out of bed to do her morning stretches.

In the middle of her finger-to-toe stretches, a loud crash rattled her window. Startled, she almost fell over. A shadow fluttered behind her ivory curtains, so she crept to the window to look outside. To her surprise, though she shouldn't have been surprised, a crow was innocently looking back at her from a tree branch. She could've sworn it was smiling but blamed her weird vision on her sleepiness. Also due to her sleepiness, she opened her window and made small-talk with the bird.

"Why do you keep flying into windows?"

"*Squawk.*"

"Do you need glasses?"

The bird squawked in response as if defending itself.

As she petted the bird, it tipped its beak as if to bow thankfully.

"I'm talking to a bird. I'm petting a bird. Totally normal," Willow muttered.

"Is everything okay?" she heard her father say, followed by a light knock on her door.

She closed her eyes tightly, praying he wouldn't open the door. She was confident that if he found her petting a crow, he'd ask questions that she wasn't prepared to answer. "Everything is just peachy."

"I heard a bang," he said, concerned, as he cracked open the door.

"I dropped my book. It's fine," she yelled back and then heard her father's heavy steps move away. She stopped petting the bird, closed the window, and trudged downstairs to get something to eat, considering she had a few hours to waste before meeting the ever-so-mysterious Evander.

Her house was running low on food: only had a half-eaten box of waffles, a few cans of tomato soup, some bags of popcorn, and various vegetables in the fridge left to eat. She figured she could eat a bowl of soup or make waffles, but neither option sounded appetizing, and she wasn't in a desperate mood.

She poked her head into the hallway. "Do either of you wanna go out for breakfast somewhere?"

"You can go," her mother yelled back.

Willow changed into socially acceptable daytime clothing-a ripped pair of jeans and a t-shirt she bought as a souvenir from a family trip to Los Angeles-and called Zan to ask if he wanted to have breakfast with her since he didn't work in the mornings. She was secretly worried about what Evander was planning to show her, and why he made it seem like it was super important and life changing.

Zan answered her call brightly, as he usually did.

"What are you doing?" she asked.

"I'm watching Saturday morning cartoons."

"Do you think you can skip the cartoons and have breakfast with me?"

"I don't know...they're pretty funny."

"Zan. I'm hungry."

"Give me thirty minutes. I'll pick you up."

"I'll give you twenty minutes."

He hung up.

She waited for him on the sofa with a book in her hands and eyes glued to its pages when she got a text from Zan. He was in front of her house. She grabbed a sweater from the coat closet by the front door, ran out of her house, and jumped into the passenger seat of Zan's car. She heard a bell ring but didn't see a bell anywhere. Judging by the direction he drove, he was taking her to Clara's, a cute vintage-themed diner at the end of the Art District. A small-statured woman named Barbra owned it. She'd named the diner after her daughter, Clara, who worked there as a cook.

"Thank you, sir," Willow said to Zan as he opened the door at Clara's for her.

"Of course, dear madam." He bowed respectfully. They sat at a table in the center of the restaurant. Barbra wasn't waitressing, but another woman greeted them with menus and mugs of freshly brewed coffee. She was just as nice as Barbra.

"Are you meeting that guy tonight?" Zan asked while stirring sugar into his coffee with a fork.

"I'm more than sure I will."

Zan picked up a menu.

She smiled. He wasn't typically a jealous friend, but jealousy was the vibe she got from him as he flipped through the menu. She saw his eyes darting from dish to dish. He wore his favorite purple-tinted contacts, but he always wore them, opting out of glasses because, according to him, none framed his face well enough. She had seen the actual brown color of his eyes only a small number of times.

"He's like the white rabbit." Willow slid her menu to the edge of the table. "He caught my curiosity."

"Do you find him attractive?" Zan put down his menu.

Willow laughed. "I don't know. Does that matter?"

"Don't avoid the question."

"I haven't thought about it," she said. Evander

was attractive, at the very least, his striking blue eyes; she had to give him that much. But he was also creepy, and in her book, creepy overpowered attractive. Zan's caring about her opinion of Evander's looks felt odd to her, since he knew she didn't judge people by their exteriors.

"Do *you* find him attractive, Zan?" Willow sipped her coffee teasingly.

He shrugged and shot her a bashful look.

She grinned at him and playfully kicked his ankle with her foot under the table. There was something much deeper going on with Zan, and she wanted badly to know what that something was. She was far too nosey to let Zan's out-of-place comments and questions slide by her.

She ordered chocolate filled crepes, and Zan ordered a classic and slightly boring cheese omelet.

"You're gonna tell me what happens tonight, right?" Zan asked with his mouth full.

Willow giggled. "Of course, if I don't die first."

"Do you want *me* to take you to that address he gave you? I would feel more comfortable knowing where you'll be."

"That would be nice. Thank you."

"Do your parents know where you're going?"

"No, and to be honest, I hope they never find

out."

"Yikes."

Zan didn't have many friends other than Willow. He always said that he felt too intimidating to socialize with people his age, which could be taken two ways. Either he was conceited or had a very strange case of low self-esteem. She didn't find him intimidating at all, but then again, she didn't find many people who intimidated her.

After breakfast, she and Zan walked around the Art District. "Your names sound the same," she said out of the blue. "Zander and Evander. Your names are almost identical."

Zan huffed. "Only you would notice that." He bumped her with his shoulder.

"I like how similar your names sound. Brings a little familiarity, I guess."

"You have a weird perspective on things."

She rolled her eyes at that comment and shoved her hands into her pant pockets. Zan drove her back home around noon, leaving her with five agonizing hours of free time. She turned the cold front door knob and walked in to see her parents sitting on the couch, talking like nothing had even happened the night before.

"How was breakfast?" her mother chirped.

"Good."

She notified her parents that she would be leaving again later that evening, leaving out exactly where she would be going.

She was absolutely, positively stuck. Stuck between clothing choices. She didn't want to dress up too much and seem like she was trying too hard to impress, or go too casual like she barely even tried at all. It was difficult to find a middle ground between *homeless person* and *gala*. Very difficult.

Then she had to wait until the clock struck four-thirty, when she would start walking to Crossroads. *Maybe I could do the laundry*, she thought, *but there are lots of other things I could do. Like rob a bank or print out a hundred pictures of Nicolas Cage and stick them in places all over the house.* The last time she considered herself bored, her mother's rose bushes in the backyard ended up burnt down due to a homemade flamethrower. Needless to say, Willow was forbidden to own any squirt guns or lighter fluid, which was probably for the better.

She started thinking about the dream she had about the piano in the shack by the beach. After realizing that most of her dreams weren't literal, but rather symbolic, she dove into a world of introspection. She thought about every little detail in the places and things she saw while she was asleep. Then she took notice that some of her dreams were messages or keys; sometimes she would see certain aspects of her dreams in her real life soon after dreaming them. Once, she dreamt about running through a field of daisies—out of all the dreams she possibly could've had, she had to have one that looked like a commercial for air freshener—and the next week on her birthday, Zan gave her a bouquet of daisies. Though most people would've called that a coincidence, she thought it meant more, since that hadn't been the only time such a thing had happened. One dream that had stuck in the back of her brain was about the fight at her old high school. She never told anyone about the premonition. She'd rather pretend she never dreamt it in the first place.

She lost track of time and did nothing but lay on the fluffy white rug in her bedroom, munching cold pizza and staring yet again at the glow-in-the-dark stars glued to her ceiling.

Then she took a nap, which seemed like a pretty good way to pass the time.

***

Willow saw herself lying in an all-white room.

She felt as if she was in a video game and she was playing the main character. The room was empty and had a single white door. She stood up and slowly walked toward it. Once opened, she stepped onto a small patch of grass guarded by a ten-foot tall rod iron fence, resembling a cage, covered in vines with the pinkest roses she had ever seen. Maybe the vines were flustered, she thought, and the vines blushed with bloomed roses.

Then she noticed the white door she had stepped through was no longer visible. Evidently, she was stuck in that cage. The iron fence was far too tall to climb over, and the ground was far too rough and compact to dig a hole. She moved some of the vines aside so she could see through the fence. She knew she was outside, since the baby blue sky was right above her head, but when she saw she was in the middle of another field, her chest tightened in panic.

She paced back and forth, clenching her fists so tightly that her knuckles started to ache. *Wake up. Wake up.* She shut her eyes tight but she didn't wake up.

Lying down seemed like the best idea. Being stuck wasn't a new thing to her. If all else failed, she knew that falling asleep in her own dream would help her snap out of it. She focused on her body, relaxed her muscles and breathed steadily. Her hands were at both of her sides and she faced upwards. Out of frustration, she clenched her fists again, and then felt a discomforting transition.

***

Willow woke up to see her starry ceiling. She lifted herself into a sitting position and noticed that it was almost four o'clock. Time passed by so much faster in dreams. She packed a purse full of necessities: a pocketknife, pepper spray, her wallet, cell phone, and keys, and she made sure she was wearing her ruby ring, the one her mother had given her. After one last check in the mirror, she decided to head out and start walking to Crossroads.

Her parents were in the kitchen, making homemade soup together. It was only a matter of time before the project would explode into a full-blown fight. Willow used to appreciate a homemade dinner almost every night, but she started to dislike the routine, which usually ended with an argument and uneaten food thrown in the trash. Homemade meals no longer felt any more special than fast-food. She announced unenthusiastically, "I'm leaving now."

Her mother scowled at her. "Where are you going?"

Willow couldn't look at her mother and tell a lie. "Zan's...for...for a movie marathon."

Elizabeth kissed Willow's forehead. "Well, okay. Be careful."

Before leaving, Willow snuck her hand across the kitchen island and grabbed a carrot.

When she closed the door behind her, her stomach dropped. She hated lying to her parents, but she couldn't tell them what she was really going to do. They would've spent three hours lecturing her about *stranger danger*, or something along those lines. She could've avoided lying by just staying home. But of course, curiosity had taken over, and off she went, walking down the hill to Crossroads in search of excitement in her life. She often struggled with feeling like she was smart enough to make her own decisions but too young to completely go her own way. Parental guidance was truly necessary sometimes.

A lot of kids tested for their driver's licenses and received fancy cars for their birthdays. She preferred walking. Of course, if the moment called for it, she would catch a ride from someone or even take the bus, but if she had a choice, she would walk everywhere. She noticed so much more when out in the open rather than stuck in a vehicle.

As she entered Crossroads, a strange gold bell rang above the door. After seeing that nobody seemed to notice the sound, she stepped up to the counter and tapped on the familiar silver bell. Zan slipped out of the backroom and smiled nervously at her.

"What good is a bell if no one comes out when it rings?" she asked with a hint of annoyance in her tone.

"What bell?" Zan looked confused.

"The bell above the front door."

"We don't have a bell above the front door."

"Yes you do. It rang when I walked in."

Zan walked to the other side of the room and looked above the door. "I don't see any bell."

She turned to follow his gaze, and to her disbelief, there was no bell above the door. "I swear...there was a bell."

Zan looked at her as if she'd grown a second nose then yelled to the backroom. "I'm leaving. Be back in a jiffy."

Zan opened the passenger door to his car for her, saw her safely inside, and then jumped in the driver's seat. "Where are we going?"

"551 Nova Drive."

He sighed, tapped the GPS app on his phone, and typed in the address.

A woman's voice came out of the speaker. *"In one hundred yards, turn left."*

The first few minutes of the drive were awkwardly silent.

"Are you nervous?" Zan asked.

She figured he'd asked that question because she was quiet. "I'm thinking."

"About what?"

"The bell."

"You were just hearing things. I wouldn't over think it."

"But I saw it. I didn't just hear it."

"Maybe you were hallucinating." Zan focused on the road, but occasionally turned his head to look at Willow.

In her defense, she wasn't paying much attention to him. She tuned out most noises except for the voices in her head as she sorted through an extensive list of reasons why she saw a non-existent bell. Considering all she had experienced, she knew she wasn't hallucinating.

"Fairies." The word accidentally escaped her lips.

"What?"

She quickly snapped out of daydream mode.

"Did you just say fairies?"

"Did I?"

"I think you did."

"Oh," she said, embarrassed.

"You're losing it, Willow." Zan smiled.

They didn't drive much longer. The robot-sounding woman in Zan's phone said, *"You have arrived at your destination."*

"This isn't creepy at all." Zan sneered at the old apartment building he'd parked in front of. "Did he give you an apartment number?"

"No."

"How are you supposed to know where to go?"

"I'll figure it out." Willow clicked her seatbelt off and opened the car door. She sensed the worry in Zan's voice. "I'll be okay. Call you later tonight. Thanks for the ride." She shut the door.

Zan waved goodbye through the window then slowly drove away.

She faced the building and walked up to the double doors of the entrance. The hinges squeaked as she pushed her way inside. A steep, un-safe looking wooden staircase greeted her. *Great.* The wood under her feet creaked with every step she took. She felt like she was going to fall right through the stairs, but thankfully, she reached the top in one piece. She found herself in a narrow, dingy hallway with maroon wallpaper that drooped on the walls. The glass light sconces were dirty; some were broken. The apartment complex also seemed quite old, quite gross, and quite like a place drug addicts would hide out.

There were two directions she could've gone. Her instincts led her to the right, though she didn't know why. She passed door after door, resisted knocking on them and disturbing whoever might occupy the rooms. *Maybe I should just leave.* However, she reached a door at the far end of the hall. It was a different color than the others, which were just plain brown; this one was dark purple. A festive pine wreath surrounded the peephole.

Steeling her resolve, she knocked on the door and waited for a big scary wrestler type man to answer it. She saw the knob turn and suddenly felt her throat close. The door opened, but she didn't feel any better about seeing a familiar face.

"Has anyone ever pointed out how extremely punctual you are?" Evander smiled and tilted his head.

Her only answer was to spit out a simple, "No."

"Then let me be the first to tell you, Willow,

you are extremely punctual." He moved aside, extended his arm, and waited for her to step inside.

The apartment was draped in colorful orange, red, and purple silk fabrics with amazingly complex textures and patterns. Fairy lights and paper lanterns hung from the ceiling. The entire place smelled of sage from the incense he had lit. Evander had furnished his apartment with vintage pieces. A pale green settee stood out in the living room, and in front of it sat a white oval coffee table. She also noticed that all kinds of crystals were placed everywhere: amethyst, opal, quartz, and other various rocks she didn't recognize. It was a strangely comfortable place. Its character was warm and inviting, unlike her own home.

"It's loud, isn't it?" Evander stood by her, looking around the apartment.

"What is?" She turned to him, clutching the strap of her purse.

"The room. It's very loud." He walked to the left of her, into his small open kitchen where a silver teakettle whistled on the stove.

"Loud is an understatement. It *is* lovely, though."

"Would you like some tea? Its black lavender rose." He poured two mugs as if he anticipated her answer.

She nodded and walked farther into the living room. She hovered by the sofa, unsure if she was allowed to sit on it. Two blank canvases on the wall baffled her. A strange rod iron bar stretched between them.

Evander handed her a black mug and sat down, so she sat down, as well, and set her purse on the floor next to her.

She waited before taking a sip. "You didn't put poison in this, did you?"

He tilted his head. "You're not obligated to drink it."

She took a sip and was glad he'd sweetened her tea with honey. "I think we should get this over with," she said more bluntly than she intended.

"Get what over with?" He set his mug on the table.

"Show me what you wanted to show me."

"Are you in a rush?" He draped his arm on the back of the sofa.

She thought about what to say, since Evander had a witty counter response to just about anything she said...almost as if he knew what was going to come out of her mouth before she did. "I don't want to be here longer than necessary. You asked me to give you a chance to show me something, and I'm giving it to you now."

Evander stared at her. "Why so talkative..." His tone changed to a low and calm whisper, and his words trailed, like his voice was helium and floated in the air like a birthday balloon.

She realized how rude she'd sounded. Being rude was never her intention. She sunk into her seat.

He must've known he wouldn't get a response, so he rotated his body and leaned a few inches closer to her. "I believe you already have some knowledge on this subject."

She rotated her body toward him, as well. His voice mesmerized her; it drew her in. "What subject?"

"A bird has been following you, a black bird that likes to be petted like a cat."

"That's not breaking news."

"How about this?" Evander lifted his arm and snapped his fingers. That same bird flew in from another room and landed on Evander's wrist.

She choked on her tea. "What in blazes...?"

"She's a drama queen. Always waiting for her cue." He lowered his arm and started petting the bird with his free hand.

Willow shook her head in disbelief. "It's *your*

bird? *That* bird is *your* bird?"

"I do have to apologize for asking if you'd seen her before. I was reassuring myself."

"About what?"

"You."

His answer stabbed her chest with a burning hot pitchfork. She was ready to grab her purse and leave. "So you have been following me."

"I haven't. *She* has." He nodded to the bird.

He's obviously delusional. Just another one of Dr. Everly's whack-o patients.

"I'm not stalking you. The first time I ever saw you was in Eira's office, and that's the truth."

"Unless you have a good answer as to why you sent your pet to spy on me, I *will* leave, and I *will* call the cops."

Or the state mental hospital.

Evander tilted his head again. His movements seemed so feline–like. "No matter how I say this, you're going to do whatever you want, anyway. In fact, I'm debating whether I should tell you or not, whether your hostility toward me is worth it or not. I know if you listened, you would believe it's worthwhile, but you think there's no sincerity or truth in what I say. I don't blame you. It's a human instinct to distrust the improbable."

Willow scanned the room again, noticing all

the work that he put into the décor to make it look so amazing. She tried to reason with herself...and with Evander. He didn't seem like he wanted to hurt her because he could've slit her throat by now. Even so, she didn't dare put all her trust in him.

The bird flew off his wrist and perched on the iron rod between the two blank canvases.

"Why do you have unpainted pictures?" Willow asked.

"They *are* painted." Evander chuckled. He looked into her eyes, and there were those blue irises staring at her with so much confidence and winsomeness. "Maybe one day you'll see things in a better perspective."

"Who are you?" she asked, trying her best to comfort herself and loosen up. She wanted to feel her ears tingle more with the heavy music of Evander's voice. She was also getting slightly carried away. What was it about him that was so enveloping? She hadn't been in his apartment for more than a few minutes, and already she had a cup of tea, gotten angry, confused, and then intrigued again.

"I'm a good man." Evander shrugged.

Willow couldn't help but laugh, realizing he had described himself by the definition of his name. "And who am I?"

"You're a tree."

Willow laughed again. "Of course, a Willow tree." She thought he was clever.

They shared a comfortable silence.

She took a moment to look at the person sitting next to her, that strange, tall, weird person who emitted so much charm. She originally thought he couldn't have had a negative bone in his body, but of course, that couldn't have been true. Everyone had a bad side, and everyone had baggage. But not everyone was as exhilaratingly beautiful as she saw him, not externally, but internally.

"Beautiful." Willow couldn't control her thoughts well enough for them to stay in her head where they belonged.

"What is?" Evander questioned; not her, but the word. He didn't ask her why she said the word, he asked her what she thought was beautiful, and she found that interesting. She felt guilty for never giving him a real chance to explain himself.

"Everything in this moment," she said, keeping her voice low.

Evander stood up from the sofa and walked into the kitchen.

She could hear rattling noises, and then a

drawer closing.

"Do you believe in the paranormal?" he asked as he returned to the sofa.

"I suppose I do." She yawned. It wasn't late in the day, but Evander was so calm, he relaxed her too much.

"Then you must believe that we are not just flesh, blood, and bones. We are spirits."

"It's a really interesting idea."

He smiled. "There are three classes of spirits, each having their own levels: *Commons*, *Idios*, and *Omnipotents*."

"I've never heard of anything like that."

"Our bodies are tin foil wrappers around chocolate bars. The outside is shiny and smooth, but on the inside is something so much better, but you can't know the flavor of chocolate until you peel away the wrapper. Dr. Everly really hasn't brought any of this to your attention, has she?"

"I don't see Dr. Everly. My mother does."

A mischievous smile spread across Evander's face. "May I ask you something?"

She nodded yes even though she wanted to ask all the questions.

He put his hand up to Willow's cheek. "Can you keep your eyes on mine?" His voice was extremely low and breathy.

His attitude shifts were throwing her off, but she listened. Her ability to blink automatically ceased, which made her nervous, but not nervous enough to jump up and stop whatever it was that he was doing to her.

He shut his eyes. "When I open my eyes, keep staring into them. Help me count to three. One."

"Two," she breathed.

"Three." Evander's eyes fluttered open. His pupils covered his irises like black holes.

She felt as if all the oxygen was sucked out of her lungs. In one millisecond, she blinked and his pupils were back to normal, but the color in his irises was swirling. They looked like the marbles she'd collected when she was a kid.

He slowly took his hand off her cheek and set it on her shoulder.

"What did you do...to me?" Her voice cracked and she felt suddenly weak. She wanted to throw up, or cry, or crawl in a hole and die. She covered her mouth with her hand and looked around in astonishment. She and Evander were now in a four-walled room, painted black. There were eight windows, two on each wall, with only the glass shielding them from the pitch-black night. The room was dim, lit only by a floor lamp in the far left corner. Directly in the center of the room stood a shiny black piano. Evander sat with her on its matching black bench.

"Where are we?" Evander sounded sedate.

A knot tightened in her throat. "What did you do?"

"This place isn't familiar to you?" Evander traced his fingers on the piano keys.

She was speechless.

"Usually we go to a place you know or somewhere you recently thought about. So it's strange that you don't—"

"No," she interrupted him. "I've been here before. I dreamt about this place last night."

Evander played a G chord on the piano. "There, see, now *that* makes sense." He played several other chords before asking, "Do you know how to play?"

"I don't...I don't understand what's happening." Her head felt like it was going to explode. She wanted answers. Her mind came to a standstill. She was too freaked out to think about rational reasons for how she ended up in the room she had only dreamt about. She thought that maybe Evander had spiked her tea with some kind of drug.

"Play with me." He picked up her hand and set her fingers on the keyboard.

"I don't know how to play." Willow's responses came naturally, almost as if her instincts were trying to tell her that she was okay, and that deep down, she knew what was happening.

Evander turned away from her and started playing something bright and happy. His fingers moved from note to note quickly and weightlessly. His body swayed with each beat. He closed his eyes and played effortlessly.

She was mesmerized by how in tune he was, even if she thought he'd drugged her, causing her to have bizarre hallucinations of not only him but also the piano and the song. She noticed he was only playing the high notes, since he was on the right side.

"Play with me," Evander commanded.

This time, she didn't question his request. She put both her hands on the lower note keys and counted her fingers. There were five on each hand. She wasn't dreaming. She thought that if she was hallucinating and confused, she could at least try to make the best of the situation.

The perks of being an optimist, she mocked herself.

She tried to feel the fun, bouncy beat in the tips of her fingers and hit a single key, luckily matching his. Evander's lips curved into a proud smile. He ended the song and set his hands on the keys, matching hers.

"Don't focus on the technicalities. Focus on the sound, the music, focus on yourself."

As hard as she tried to bottle up how scared she was, her nerves prickled her stomach and tears coated her eyes. "I can't do this. I want to go home. Please take me home." She choked on the words she couldn't swallow back into her throat.

"You can do this."

She looked down at her hands and started to bounce her fingers back and forth between a few keys, which created a simple and soft melody.

Evander matched chords with her melody.

Chills ran down her arms due to a cold, quick breeze. She thought it must've been a draft, but then realized, *there are no drafts in heaven.* Even though, sometimes, she doubted she was the type of person who would go to heaven because of how often she gave in to the devil tugging at the collar of her shirt. She listened to the fallen angel as if she had forgotten everything Sunday school taught her as a young child.

She and Evander played slowly. She toyed around with notes, and Evander followed along with her. They played. She played; just like she did in her dream. Little by little, she felt her body loosen. Her eyelids were sticking together, making it that much harder for her to open her eyes again. It took a lot of energy to open her eyes, but when she did, she turned to her left and saw that she was again in Evander's apartment. He was rustling around in the kitchen, pushing microwave buttons, taking down plates from cupboards and tearing off paper towels from a roll.

Her heart felt heavy in her chest. She had just fallen asleep, and everything she'd experienced was just another dream...but no; she had counted five fingers... She had so many questions that she wasn't sure she should address Evander about them, or how to address them at all, for that matter. He'd certainly doubt her sanity.

Evander whistled as he opened the microwave and took out two paper-towel-wrapped blueberry muffins. He set each one on a clean plate. From what she could see, the little color he had in his face and lips dulled out. The thick curls that were sticking out from the top of his head had all fallen onto his forehead. She wondered if that was how he always looked, as she'd never really noticed before, or if his appearance really did suddenly go somber. He poured more tea into their mugs and placed both hands on the counter top, throwing his head forward. She felt oddly concerned about him, but he straightened up again quickly and took the two mugs to the living room, placing them both on the table.

"Tea for you, tea for me," he said and turned back to grab the two plates of muffins, which he also placed on the table. He sat heavily on the sofa, and this time leaned his head back with his arms crossed at his chest.

She studied the steam coming from the hot tea, wishing he had at least put some sugar or honey in hers like he did before. Tea was too bitter without any form of sweetener. She sat up from her slumped position. "Are you okay?"

"Tired." He turned to look at her. "Are *you* okay?" He bobbed his head toward her, a smile on his face.

"What happened?" She grabbed a mug and took a sip of the tea, fighting to remain composed. "Did I fall asleep?"

"Something like that." A long breath trailed behind the words he whispered. He reached over and tore a piece off his muffin, and then threw it quickly into his mouth. "What I'd like to know...why aren't you kicking or screaming. Why aren't you crying or running out of here yelling for help?"

She didn't want to remind herself of how tired she was. Tired of the false assumptions and being asked *why* so often.

"Why are you quiet?"

"Why do you think so much?"

She should've been the one asking *why*. *Why* did it seem like people were always looking for reasons to ask *why?*

Evander leaned closer to her and looked deeply into her eyes. "The minute you took my hand, you knew you would see me again, and you knew things were going to change."

"Who are you to assume that?" she countered.

Another voice answered, "He's someone I should've introduced you to a long time ago." The icy voice came from the room that stupid crow flew out of and apparently flew back into. A woman with white hair and wrinkleless skin walked out of the room: her mother's psychiatrist.

"Everly," Willow whispered the doctor's last name. She couldn't believe that Dr. Eira Everly, of all people, was standing in front of her. Weird things happened all the time: finding money on the ground after giving some to the homeless, or getting a phone call from the person she was thinking about only seconds before. Willow didn't know if Dr. Everly's presence in Evander's apartment should have been considered a *weird* thing, or a scary, pass-out worthy thing. She thought both, definitely both.

"Glad I could skip the introduction between you two." Evander got up from the sofa and walked behind Dr. Everly, sliding both his hands over her shoulders.

"I hope you don't mind the interruption," Everly said, "but Evander really needs to learn how to get to the point of things."

"I like to explain myself," he said in his defense.

Dr. Everly pulled away from Evander's grip and faced him. "Could you possibly learn to explain yourself without wasting your energy on traveling through realities and mind controlling this poor girl into trusting you?"

"I didn't mind control her, Eira. Not everyone who trusts me is being mind-controlled."

"What about Aveda? Or Orion maybe? How about—?"

"Five times, Eira. I've used that control five times. Can we get past that, please?"

"I don't mean to interrupt," Willow muttered, awkwardly sitting in the same spot on the sofa and unsure of what to do or say, or whether she should say or do anything at all.

"I'm still human." Evander smirked and walked into his kitchen where he rummaged through his fridge.

Eira sat softly where Evander sat previously. Dr. Everly looked ghostly. She looked frightening. Willow always thought that Dr. Everly looked like she could be part of some royal family or that she was just rich, very rich, with her satin dresses and pearls around her neck and wrists. Willow couldn't take her eyes off of the woman. She was trying to put together pieces of the weird puzzle in front of her, but none of the pieces were fitting together. They were all too oddly shaped.

"My Willow, you look like you've just seen a ghost," Eira said in a mocking tone.

"Are you a ghost?"

"Don't you worry, I'm not dead. Not right now, anyway. Evander on the other hand—"

"Enough," Evander interrupted her. He carried three small plates, each one with several slices of various cheeses. "What do you need, Eira?"

Dr. Everly tilted her head at him. "I need to get things moving. Don't question my authority. Just because you haven't scared this young girl away with your behavior, doesn't mean you're any more important to her than you were."

Evander clenched his jaw and moved some of

the hair out of his face. He sat next to Dr. Everly on the sofa's armrest. "It seems as though Dr. Everly hasn't eaten her evening serving of bread crust, making her just a little cranky and egoistic." Evander glanced at the doctor and back at Willow.

"It also seems as though Evander may need to take a minute to think about how much he's putting his life at risk." Dr. Everly never moved her eyes away from Willow's. "And yours, too, my dear."

Willow realized she'd landed in the middle of a domestic argument. They were like a married couple, throwing insults and threats back and forth. They could be her parents. It was actually nerve-racking, considering how both Evander and Dr. Everly seemed to have a lot of power in the palms of their hands. According to the doctor, Evander was misusing his power. Willow, of course, was not one to decide whether that was true or not. She hadn't known Evander long enough. She quickly turned away from Eira's deadening gaze and grabbed her purse from its place on the floor. When she turned back, instead of Dr. Everly sitting next to her, a black crow stood in her place.

Fighting panic, and trying to contain herself, Willow shot up from the couch. "It's t-time for me to go." The shakiness in her voice was unfortunate, but as the night had progressed, her emotions finally overloaded her self-control.

"I'll drive you." Evander got up from the armrest, grabbed his keys off the hook by the door, led her out, and followed her down the steep stairs. They reached the sidewalk and turned to each other.

"I'm sorry, Evander. You're just too much excitement for me."

He looked up at the sky. The sun was already gone, being about eight o'clock in the evening. "How would you like to go to the park? Let's unwind a bit, or you'll never get a wink of sleep."

She answered him with a nod, not knowing why she agreed to go anywhere with him in the first place. Mind control? Curiosity? Stupidity?

He took her hand and led her to the back of the building. One of the many things her parents had taught her was to never follow a strange person into a dark alley or a place where no other people—witnesses—were around. But this person wasn't strange. Well, he was, but there was something about him that was familiar and comfortable. He had a way of soothing her angst. She considered the idea that she was under his spell, but then questioned herself about that possibility. She was not a weak-minded person. A lot of things seemed impossible to her then, walking only a foot behind that strange person who only knew and did strange things. She then thought that if her parents knew where she was, she'd be grounded for life.

As she was deep in thought, he let go of her hand and unlocked the passenger door of a light turquoise convertible sports car. It had white leather interior that sparkled under the intense moonlight.

"Nice car." Willow was scared to even touch the door handle.

"Sure is." Evander climbed into the driver's seat and waited for her to get in, as well. No chivalry lost on him, for sure. She eventually opened her own door and got in, but not until after basking in the beauty of such a glorious car. Not a lot of people around Rosaphene took this much care of their vehicles.

The car ride to the park was silent but short. The minute they arrived at Rosaphene Park, Evander lit up excitedly again. He opened Willow's door for her and they walked with their hands in their pockets, looking for a nice place on the grass to sit. They picked a spot near a bridge that stretched across a shallow lake. Rosaphene

Park, in the spring and summer, was strictly a paid-use campground. But in the fall and winter, the park was open to everyone for free. Tonight, some pretty disturbing people loitered around.

She and Evander lay down next to each other on the grass and looked up at the sky, staring at the stars like she used to do quite frequently. Evander turned his head to look at her, but she didn't look back. She was too busy admiring the universe, an endeavor she hadn't made the time to do after graduating high school. It seemed as though the more time she had on her hands, the less often she did the things she loved to do.

"What's your favorite constellation?" he asked.

She thought about that for a second. Her favorite constellation usually changed as the seasons changed. "Draco. Dragons symbolize success, luck, and power. Things that a lot of people want, but not many have."

He shifted positions, as if bracing himself for what was to come. "I'm in the third level of Omnis. I'm a *Numinist*, a spirit guide."

Willow's nervousness resurfaced. After looking at him, he seemed fairly normal, fairly human, fairly safe to be around, but he was talking like a crazy person. "What's all this got to do with me?"

"You're feeling something that you've never felt before." He paused to take a deep breath. "It's been said that there is a bond that can't be broken between witches and their *familiar spirits*. There is also a similar bond between Numinists and their destined Looscents...when they meet, if their meeting ever happens in the first place."

Willow had no idea what he was talking about and considered interrupting, but she liked the sound of his voice so she let him prattle on.

"Each Looscent roaming this earth has a guide, a Numinist. Experienced Numinists have been reincarnated many times. Every generation, a handful of Looscents are born, and the reincarnation of a Numinist occurs closely before the birth of a new Looscent, without fail. The numbers are always even, giving each meeting more of a chance to occur, but the meetings don't always happen, nor do they have to happen. It's up to destiny. However, I'm sad to say...these meetings are becoming rare. The number of Numinists and Looscents has been dropping. There have been some disturbances and...some murders. Idios, who are the second class of spirits, are also targeted. But we can save that discussion for another day. I don't want to overwhelm you."

Too late.

"Just be assured we were destined to meet."

Willow pondered everything he had told her. She contemplated her life, and life in general. She felt that, had Evander been right, if she hadn't been dreaming or seeing things, none of what he revealed was bad news. In fact, it would've been the greatest news she'd heard in a long time. Finding out that all of the theories, ideas, and stories about spirituality and the afterlife were true, she'd have something the majority of people didn't have: answers. She worried that she had taken everything a bit too lightly but questioned how someone was supposed to handle knowing the secrets of the universe. Should she scream them from rooftops? Who would believe her? Dr. Everly would, for sure.

"How do you know Dr. Everly?"

"Longtime friend. She's also a Numinist. A tad more experienced than I, but just a tad."

"She's a freaking crow. What's that all about?" Willow's phone rang. It was Zan, probably worried that she hadn't answered any of the many texts he'd sent her. She didn't answer her phone, not wanting to go back to the weird reality of Cinnamon Lattes and conflict at home. Not wanting to remember that what she was doing with Evander was ignorant and dangerous in other people's eyes. Even if everything was okay, there would always be the, *"Why?"*

"Why did you lie to your parents?"

"Why are you letting your curiosity take over your logic?"

"Why are you hanging out with Evander?"

"I'm tired," she told him.

"We'll continue this some other time."

He drove her to the corner of the street where she lived, and they exchanged quiet goodbyes. Evander promised to talk to her soon. He had to discuss things with Dr. Everly first, before he could explain what's even farther down the rabbit hole...what was in store for her next.

Willow took it in stride, answered, "Okay." *My life's going to be normal again...tomorrow morning. I don't have to worry about my future right now.* Clarence had told her that destiny would inspire her. Everything would turn out the way it was meant to be. She promised herself not to Google any of the spirit names Evander used, or over-think them too much. She did have a life, and Evander had barely entered it.

She took her usual deep breath before unlocking her home's front door. When she walked in, she smelled chicken broth and didn't realize how hungry she was, but she decided against eating anything. She needed to sleep a few hours...or perhaps years; years sounded too good to be true.

She slept without interruption that night.

Chapter 2
TRUTH OR CONSEQUENCES

Willow woke up feeling the same way she had felt in eighth grade when she went to school with a stomach virus: tired, heavy, and nauseous. Thankfully, she hadn't thrown up all over the students in art class. This time, she threw up in her bathroom sink and slumped down under it, leaning her head on the cabinet, hoping that she wouldn't completely pass out. It took a while to see colors normally again, because they all looked neon-like, as if she had taken some kind of drug that made her hallucinate. However, what had happened the night before had been no illusion, no dream. She had counted her fingers. It was all very real, leaving her both physically and emotionally drained.

The aftershock of that night was strange and nothing like she had ever been through before. She spent most of her early morning curled up in a ball in bed with a headache and severe nausea.

She contemplated telling her mother about how bad she felt, but Elizabeth would start asking her questions, and she wasn't up to telling more lies. Avoiding her parents as much as possible that day seemed to be the best option.

She quietly snuck down the stairs, into the kitchen, and looked through cabinets and drawers, in desperate need of pain relievers. The house was way too quiet to be nine-thirty in the morning. After popping an aspirin in her mouth and gulping down half a bottle of water, she searched every room in the house, but her parents were nowhere to be found. They had left no notes or given her any verbal notice that they would be gone. She decided to call her parents around noon, just to make sure they were okay.

Willow heard her phone ring from her bedroom. She didn't bother running upstairs to answer it because she knew she wouldn't make it in time. Her phone rang until she was halfway up the stairs, climbing them with difficulty as she had to keep from stepping wrong and tumbling down. On the way to her room, she knew being hit by an eighteen-wheel truck wouldn't make her feel as sick and broken as she felt now.

Zan had texted her three times. She sat on the edge of her bed and ran her hand through her hair, and then called him back.

"Good morning, Zan." Her voice was almost all gone. She sounded like she had been smoking.

"Were you planning on telling me what happened last night?" he snapped. "Or do I have to pry it out of you?"

"I don't want to talk about it."

"That bad, huh?" Zan sounded solemn. He seemed dissatisfied with her reluctance to talk but let her have her peace. "I'm here for you any time you want to talk."

Willow wanted to go back to sleep. She, of course, wasn't planning on telling Zan the whole truth. She didn't know how sane any of her explanations would sound. Sooner or later, white lies were bound to turn black.

Hours passed until the clock struck noon. Willow's headache went away but she still felt weak and sick to her stomach. Her parents wouldn't answer her phone calls, so out of desperation she called Zan back. "Have you heard from my parents?"

"No. What's wrong?"

"Can you come over?"

"Be right there."

Whereas most things she was able to handle, whatever Evander did to her made her tolerance level drop and anxiety escalate. Everything seemed like a big deal. Her perception was already changing, but she hadn't realized the scope and depth of it yet.

***

Zan rushed to Willow's house. He had been getting ready to start his shift at Crossroads earlier than usual, so he was wearing old jeans and a coffee-stained white shirt. Willow had asked him why he insisted on wearing that shirt instead of buying a new one. He had said that the stain made him look serious about his job, and artsy. She had rolled her eyes at his excuses.

Zan liked his routines. He liked waking up at the same time every day, wearing the same clothing, eating the same junk for dinner. Evander blowing into town, causing Willow distress and interrupting his routine, was something Zan wasn't handling very well.

He knew where the Ferring family kept one of their spare keys, in case of an emergency. Willow's parents were nice to him. They liked to hear that she associated with *mature*, goal-orientated people. Willow would laugh at that because neither of them fell into the *mature* category.

To the left of the door grew a nice plant with

big leaves; he was pretty sure it was a croton but never asked Willow or her mother. Her father didn't seem like the plant-buying type. The key was taped to the back of one of the leaves. Zan searched for a leaf that seemed heavier than the others and found the key. After unlocking the front door, he found Willow sitting cross-legged on the sofa with a blanket around her.

When he stepped inside the house, he could *feel* Evander's presence, his energy strongly emitting from Willow. Zan worked hard to rid himself of that energy. It made him feel sickly, knowing that Evander already had Willow wrapped around his finger. He had a tendency to ruin people's lives, or at least, a tendency to ruin the lives of people he loved. Zan didn't want to blame everything on Evander, but he was too hurt not to.

***

"For a minute there, I thought you were my dad." Willow tilted her head at Zan, like Evander tilted his head at her.

Zan locked the door behind him. He walked to the sofa and sat next to her then surprised her with a tight hug.

He hid his face in her dark knotted hair. She let

herself fall into the hug. Willow felt confused, lonely and a little scared, which Zan knew without her saying a word. A lot of good people didn't get enough credit or recognition for being good, and Zan was one of those people, without a doubt. He gave Willow the company and quietness she needed. He allowed her to rest, and he played with her hair as they watched television until Zan spoke up.

"Willow." He looked down at her and hoped she wouldn't take what he had to say wrong. "I really want to give you space, but first I want you to tell me about last night."

She sat up and turned her body to face Zan so she wouldn't have to strain to look at him. He wasn't wearing his purple contacts. "Evander thinks I'm...I don't know. A spirit. He's vague...but intuitive."

"Now *you're* being vague."

"If a stranger invited you to his house and served you tea and crumpets then told you strange things about the world, you wouldn't be able to describe it properly. I remained calm through it all, like I understood everything, but what happened last night is beyond words."

"Did he really serve you crumpets?" Zan was on the verge of laughing, but only out of nervousness, not because he found the situation amusing.

They exchanged looks of worry.

Zan shrugged and bit his lip to keep himself from asking too many questions at once. "Do you plan to see him again?"

She felt the need to defend him. "He's close friends with my mother's psychiatrist. I don't know how to talk about this without making you think I'm crazy...or that he's crazy."

"He is crazy." Zan's voice was matter-of-fact emotionless.

It was weird to see him so facially blank.

"You're young and naïve," he went on. "You're letting this guy melt your brain with his creepy...whatever it is he's telling you about the world." Zan diverted eye contact. "I haven't met him, but I don't trust him. If you're not careful, you're going to get yourself into something you can't get out of."

"What do you think I'm going to do with him? Drive off into the sunset? Have his babies? Conjure up Satan? I'm listening to what he has to say. I don't know him but there's this weird understanding, like he's controlling my mind, making me trust him."

Controlling my mind to make me trust him. That

line repeated itself over and over in her head. She wondered if Dr. Everly was right when she accused him of doing so.

"Just *talk* to me," Zan pleaded. "You used to push me away because you're scared of getting too attached to people. Please don't go back to doing that. I'm your *friend*."

"You're making this out to be more than it is. I'm trying to find myself and I'm trying to figure out what I want to do with my life because, Zan, I don't know."

They shared another silence. She didn't like admitting that she didn't know what she wanted to do with her life. She liked to make people think she had it all together, but she didn't. Except for astrology, nothing had drawn enough of her interest for her to study one particular subject. She wasn't passionate about the medical field or going to law school. Art was never where she excelled, and sports were definitely out of the question. It was scary to be so young but feel as though a clock was ticking somewhere, and time was running out for her to pick a *path*.

"I can't tell you what to do," Zan whispered. "But I can tell you to be careful. It's better not to screw around with someone who's controlling your mind." He said the last sentence a little too confidently, but she didn't question him. She leaned into the crook of his neck and inhaled the green-apple scent of shampoo in his hair, wishing he wouldn't worry so much about her.

The rest of the day fell stagnant. Zan left at around four to get to work. Willow was very concerned about her parents' whereabouts. She paced the living room, calling her father, calling her mother, and then calling her father again. That cycle repeated for another hour until her mother finally picked up.

"What's wrong, Willow? I have a dozen missed calls from you."

Willow felt relieved but angry. "Why didn't you tell me you were leaving?"

"We did, honey. You even told us to have a nice time."

Willow's headache returned at maximum strength. "I don't remember—"

"I swear on my life. We woke you to tell you we were leaving."

"Where are you now?" Willow managed.

"Your father and I had a meeting with Dr. Everly."

"What? Everly? Why?"

"We discussed the possibility of her seeing you."

"Mother...no—"

"She's very thrilled with that idea. We'll be home soon."

The call clicked off.

Willow stared at her phone and tried her hardest to recall her mother walking into her room that morning. She couldn't help but think about how uncanny it was that Dr. Everly and her parents had a meeting. That couldn't result in good news. She was confident that Evander and Dr. Everly were conspiring together, taking advantage of Elizabeth's eagerness for Willow to talk about her dreams and whatever else her mother thought needed talking about. The less the old crow Everly knew about her, the better.

Her parents got home thirty minutes later.

"*Mother*, what did you decide in the meeting with Everly?"

"We discussed times and dates to get you in. She wants to see you three times a week."

"Oh, no."

Dr. Everly was up to something, and Willow's parents were remarkably oblivious. The longer she could keep them away from the truth, the better. She needed to deal with the doctor herself, find out what she was up to, her and Evander. Willow had a feeling, though, that everything would've ended as quickly as it had started, if that was what she wanted.

***

The next day, while resting up for her appointment with Dr. Everly, Willow heard the all-too-familiar crow, Dr. Everly herself, crash into Willow's window again.

She opened the window. "What's wrong with you?" she exclaimed to her feathered nemesis, now perched on a nearby branch.

The bird squawked at her.

"Want some pizza?" She retrieved a piece of crust from the box and offered it to the pesky bird.

Crow Everly snatched it in her beak and flipped to the ground.

Willow put her head into her hands in frustration. Until six o'clock, the bird stayed on her windowsill, just watching her. She was on the verge of downing an entire bottle of sleeping pills, because death would've probably been a whole lot easier to deal with than the crow's prying black eyes. Of course, she didn't take the pills, not only because she didn't own any, but because the thought of falling asleep and never waking up didn't seem so appealing, after all. She was glad she didn't make rash decisions.

That night, she didn't dream at all, which was great because dreams took a lot of energy out of her. She woke up early with no problems getting out of bed, for once actually feeling refreshed and ready for a new day.

"Make sure to be respectful," Elizabeth told her as they walked into Dr. Everly's office and took their seats in the waiting room. "She's here to help you." A few minutes after they'd made themselves comfortable on the antique chairs, Evander walked in with a little extra bounce in his step. He stood in front of her without saying anything, making faces to try and cause a stir.

"What are you doing here?" Willow demanded.

"You look like you've seen a ghost."

"Shut up."

Her mother looked around. "Who are you talking to, Willow?"

"Evander. He was here the other day. Remember?" Willow pointed to him.

"He's not here." Elizabeth shook her head. "Willow, there's no one here."

"He's standing right there," Willow shouted.

Evander looked at her and winked, walked past them, straight into Dr. Everly's office without opening the door.

"Oh my god," Willow mumbled to herself, feeling dizzy and nauseous. Reality didn't seem real anymore. She felt like she was walking a road with no end. A road paved with nails and rust and shards of glass, all pricking her bare feet.

When Dr. Everly interrupted her thought process and waved her into her office, Willow walked in and, immediately, her eyes went straight to Evander, who was sitting on a chair in front of Dr. Everly's desk. Willow was so emotional she ignored the sound of a small bell ringing.

When no one said anything within the first five seconds, she asked, "Do either of you want to explain what's going on?"

"You're evolving," Evander chimed in. "It's what happens when a Looscent completes the first step in training. The first step was meeting me."

"If this is your way of explaining things, you aren't doing a very good job."

"What else do you want me to say? Things are what they are, and before things start making sense, you have to accept what you are."

"I'm not a Looscent. I'm a human being."

Dr. Everly snickered. "Now isn't the time to be defensive, *child*."

Willow was once again stuck between two

strange people while they practically fought over her.

There were ups and downs to accepting the unknown. She could, after all, get in a lot of trouble. Her life could also be at risk, and there was a chance everything she'd seen was just some kind of magician's trick or game. Maybe Dr. Everly was conducting a psychological experiment on human behavior to learn how much people would believe...if she was a good enough illusionist. Whatever the case, with Clarence's prodding in the back of her mind, Willow decided to play along and took a seat next to Evander. "Okay, let me get this straight. I'm a Looscent and you're my spirit guide."

"Yup."

"How many steps are there to this training?"

He ran his fingers through his hair and sighed heavily. "I can't say exactly how many steps there are. It all depends on how willing you are to take chances. To be honest with you, it could take your whole life to complete." His face drained of color, making him look ill or dead.

Willow gulped. "What happens after?"

"After you die?"

"No, after training."

Evander eyed her like he was peering into her

soul. "In your next life, you would no longer be a Looscent. You'd be at my level, a Numinist." Evander smiled and shrugged casually, as if he'd had this exact conversation a million times before.

Dr. Everly stared at them with a look of annoyance. She folded her hands on her desk, leaned forward, and squinted at Willow. "If you wish to pass on training and continue living as an average Common spirit, you absolutely have that choice."

"No," Evander snapped and looked Dr. Everly dead in the eyes. "You know she can't do that. It's too dangerous for her to just live as an average person, *especially* right now...with the murders, and all."

"Evander, you always want to force your Looscents into training. We are no longer living in the seventeen-hundreds. Willow has a choice."

"She needs to know she could be a target." He sat up straight and pointed at Willow. "She could *die*, Eira." He looked like he was about to strangle Dr. Everly, judging by his clenched jaw.

"She could die either way, Evander."

Willow was through with being talked about like she wasn't in the room. She wanted real answers. She wanted to know what she was supposed to do.

"Why would the killer be interested in me?" Willow made sure to keep her voice level and steady. She didn't want to end up arguing with either Evander or Dr. Everly.

Dr. Everly leaned back in her seat and folded her arms across her chest. She didn't look pleased with Evander, but she never looked pleased. "You haven't told her, have you?"

He licked his teeth. "Remember how I mentioned that the numbers of Numinists and Looscents have been dropping?" He glanced quickly at Dr. Everly, and then looked at Willow with dread in his eyes. "Looscents and Idios are being murdered for their souls. That's why you're in danger."

"Who's killing them...er...us?"

"We don't know."

"Since these spirits occupy human bodies, they're *real people*, right? Have you reported the killings to the police?"

"They're as baffled as we are." Evander clenched his jaw. "It's complicated."

"Since I'm one of these spirits too, I deserve to know why it's complicated."

He sighed. "Yes, technically, every spirit, no matter the class, is a human being. But if we die this unnatural death, we completely cease to exist.

The dead spirit's parents would be unaffected by the loss, as if the murder victim was never born. It's the same concept of traveling back into the past. You inadvertently change something that affects the future drastically. Idios and Omnipotents are orbs of energy that occupy human flesh, as are Commons, though they don't have much power."

Willow paced the room, trying to understand the new information. "What about a natural death, like getting old and your body wearing out, what happens then?"

"If you die a trained Looscent, you are a first incarnation, *created* or *chosen* by the Deity, don't ask me how. You'll be reborn a Numinist, and in your next lifetime, you will have a destined Looscent to train. Numinists are reincarnated over and over from then on. However, if Looscents don't complete their training in their first lifetime, they do not get reincarnated. The Deity throws them into another realm for defective spirits."

"Wonderful." Willow looked up at the ceiling and closed her eyes. She imagined what her parents' lives would've been like if she had never been born. She knew that they would've divorced soon after they got married. Her father would've probably ended up re-marrying sometime after, while her mother would have trouble just going on a single date. She thought that her father would've liked to live in New York City, somehow he'd have a penthouse, and her mother would've lived somewhere near a beach. Willow wondered if her parents could've been happier if she never existed. Their lives would've been a lot easier, at the very least.

Willow pulled back her hair and twisted it into a bun. In a short span of time, she postponed her ultimate and final decision on whether or not she would trust Evander. "So if I were to agree to training, what would be the next step?"

Evander looked relieved and Dr. Everly looked far more frustrated than she originally had. Willow made a mental note to ask Evander why he and Dr. Everly seemed like they wanted to throw each other off a cliff all the time.

Evander's lips curled into a reassuring smile. "I'd love to introduce you to Rowan. She's an Idio who specializes in transporting. She is extraordinary, and I think you would get along well. I'm the only person who can physically train you. That doesn't mean you can't absorb information from others."

Willow nodded and felt exhilarated about doing something with her life that was risky and exciting. She felt like a rebellious teenager who played with fire and stole packets of gum from gas stations. Also, strangely, she felt like an apprentice to a mad scientist. She wasn't technically rebelling against her parents or rebelling against any system. She was rebelling against everything religion had taught her, rebelling against what science had already discovered about humanity, and she felt pretty great about stepping out of the light and into the shadows of what the rest of the world had yet to, or possibly never would, discover.

"When can we get started?" She wanted to start that very minute.

Evander looked her up and down. "How about this evening?"

"Yes," she replied without thinking twice.

Dr. Everly gritted her teeth and swiftly rose from her chair. The doctor looked sickly thin, like an elegant corpse straight out of a horror film, even more so when she wore all black. *Dr. Everly might be going to her own funeral.*

The doctor strode to the only window in her depressing office and looked as if she was studying the molecules in the air outside. Her expression was blank. "Don't screw this up, Evander."

"You have no trust in me, Eira," he stated without turning his head. "I cannot express enough how sad that makes me."

Eira turned around and stared at the back of Evander's head. "I think you should focus on more important things, rather than whether or not I trust you to train her correctly."

***

Evander and Eira Everly had a thorny relationship. He had gotten a taste of his own medicine when she betrayed him by becoming close with a man who didn't know what it meant to be kind. There was a lot that Evander knew about the universe, being dedicated to his craft and to his job, which had often gotten him in trouble. Evander disliked confessing his own mistakes and confessing that, even after centuries of existing, he didn't know everything.

Eira had been a mother figure to Evander during every one of his lifetimes. He distanced himself from the families he was born into because he had no use for them and no reason to grow close to Common spirits who didn't have anything to offer but the occasional shoulder to lean on. Family was everything, but Evander never considered his birth parents as part of his family.

Spirits he had known for marvelously long periods of time were part of his family. He hoped Willow would become part of this family and fill in the spot someone left empty, someone he had royally screwed up and lost. Evander wanted to feel whole again. He wanted to feel useful, successful, and stupidly delighted with life. There weren't many spirits who made him feel that way.

***

Willow left the office, knowing Evander would show up at her house sometime that evening to pick her up. He hadn't disclosed exactly where they were going, but he did say that he would be taking her to meet Rowan. Willow walked out of the office building with her head up, eyes focused in front of her rather than on the ground. Now there was purpose in every step she took.

As they buckled their seat-belts in the car, Willow's mother gazed at her with a sinister smirk. Willow wanted to avoid meeting her mother's stare; she wanted to avoid questions and speaking altogether. She was in a thinking mood, and attempting to engage her in conversation while she was thinking wasn't something she advised her mother to do.

As soon as her mother took her eyes off

Willow, she reversed out of the parking space and drove away. Willow created an image in her head of how she thought Rowan would look, envisioning a beauty queen of a woman, perfectly prim and proper, well-mannered and indifferent.

In Willow's peripheral vision, she caught sight of her mother putting a CD in the car's CD player. The sound of violins and cellos replaced the silence. Willow closed her eyes and let her brain become numb from the delicate strings played so effortlessly and passionately. She was the one who had convinced her mother to listen to classical music. She remembered telling her that it lowered blood pressure. Lately, her mother hardly ever listened to anything else.

"I'm going out tonight. Zan invited me to dinner." Willow's blunt statement must've sounded rude, judging by the look of disapproval Elizabeth shot her, but she made no comment.

Willow was thankful there'd be no argument.

***

Willow awaited Evander's arrival and couldn't stay focused on anything for too long. Her mind kept drifting off. She'd stare at her yellow walls for a few minutes, then out the window, then blankly at her computer screen. She'd hum the melodies of famous 80's classic rock songs and chip the polish off her nails. She wasn't often easily distracted, but the popcorn ceiling and glow stars couldn't have looked more interesting.

Willow cleaned herself up, and when she deemed herself presentable, she plopped onto the couch in the living room. She joined her mother who was watching an apocalyptic movie that had been on for an hour and a half. Willow often wondered how the world would eventually come to an end. She also wondered if the world was even going to end. Perhaps thinking the earth was somehow made to exist forever was a bit naïve, but she liked to think the planet would continue to float in space for a trillion years, long after the human species ceased to exist. She didn't think the earth would be ripped apart or explode. She liked the idea of the earth staying intact sans life and wished people wouldn't take their home-world for granted.

Her father walked in the front door. "How are my two shooting stars?" he said cheerfully. Too cheerfully.

Willow automatically thought that he must've gotten a promotion or bonus at work. "Why so chipper?"

He grinned and sat on the sofa next to Willow.

"It's a great night to stargaze. We should pull out the telescope."

"Not tonight. I'm going out."

The smile on his face faded, and he looked as shocked as if she had told him she was pregnant with a space alien's baby or Satan's spawn.

"Willow, stay home with your father tonight."

"I can't..."

"She doesn't have to stay home, Lizzy," he said. "She has a life."

"Some life she has, hanging out all day."

"Leave her alone."

"You never listen to me." Her mother stormed to her bedroom and slammed the door.

Willow and her father exchanged angry looks before he retreated to the basement. She ran outside to wait for Evander, sat on the curb, and stared up at the sky. It really was a good night to stargaze. Guilt gnawed at her insides. She fidgeted with the ruby ring on her finger and wondered whether or not she had made the right decision to rendezvous with Evander instead of spending some quality time with her father.

This might've been a golden night. Instead, it ended in a fight.

A familiar light turquoise car pulled up in front of the house across from hers. The driver flashed his headlights like Morse code. Sadly, she didn't know Morse code but assumed the message was *get in the car.* She hustled to open the passenger door.

"Are you ready to pursue your training?" Evander asked.

She buckled her belt and giggled, feeling frilly and feminine. "Are you even human, Evander?"

"Good question. Are you?"

"I haven't felt human since I met you."

"If you think feeling that way makes you special, you are thinking incorrectly. You are not a fish out of water; you are a fish in a pond but you belong in an ocean. There's a difference."

"Okay, Shakespeare."

Evander smiled and drove away from the curb. "Don't mock me."

Willow could feel how exciting her night was destined to be. She smiled and let her hair mess up in the wind as Evander sped his car down the empty streets. There was no need to make conversation with him during their ride together. She knew that they would have plenty to talk about later on that evening, after meeting Rowan.

***

Evander parked in the lot of the Rosaphene Art

Museum, which was closed for the day. Willow had only been to the museum once during a field trip in middle school. What she remembered about it wasn't exciting. It was a very small museum filled with paintings that were unimpressive. She wanted to like art, walk around galleries quietly, interpret the meaning of paintings, and analyze brush strokes, but she didn't. She hoped she would grow into liking art as she grew older. That didn't happen either.

"Don't tell me we're going to break into the art museum. I'd like to not get arrested tonight." She got out of Evander's car.

"We won't break into anywhere. Trust me."

"Every time you tell me to trust you, I feel like I trust you less."

"Your trust issues are *your* issues, not mine."

Evander led her up the many stairs leading to the main entrance of the one-story building. It was a cold night, colder than she had expected. She crossed her arms over her chest and ducked her head. The low temperature made it hard for her to tell whether she was shivering because she was cold, or because she was racked with nerves.

"Have you ever heard of The Veil between worlds?"

Willow rolled her eyes. "What do you think?"

"Of course not. Take my hand."

She intertwined her fingers with his. "I want you to close your eyes and clear your mind of anything negative."

She kept her mind steady on the thought of pomegranate seeds tossed at someone's window instead of rocks. That trope bothered her, because rocks were dangerous, especially when thrown at glass. She didn't understand how illogical the person was who came up with that idea. *At least throw rubber balls or something. There's less of chance to injure someone if a rubber ball accidentally hits their head.*

"You're going to feel a strong pull. Do not fight it. Follow it. Keep your hands and feet inside the ride at all times."

She braced herself for physical pain.

Evander squeezed her hand tight and pulled her forward.

She felt as if all the atoms in her body were separating, then re-combining, like gravity was no longer a force holding her down.

For some reason, since before she met Evander, Willow believed in angels. When she was six years old, one morning she felt a weight settle on one corner of her bed. She sat up, looked around but nothing was there. She tried going back to sleep by telling herself that she was just imagining things. But it happened again, except on the other corner of her bed. That time she didn't bother looking until she felt that weight move farther up along her bed and stop right next to her body. Her first thought was that someone must've broken into her room and she was about to become a bloodied murder victim. She may have watched too many scary movies as a child.

Willow remembered tightening her grip on her rose colored blanket and praying for the best, but then something pulled her eyelids open. She slowly focused her eyes on an ethereal figure sitting next to her. The flowing form faded out until she lost complete sight of it. Willow told herself to forget about it, that it was just a dream, but she counted five fingers on each hand. From then on, she thought she'd seen her guardian angel. She relived that experience as Evander tugged her body forward until he stopped.

"You can open your eyes now." Evander let go of her hand.

She snapped open her eyes, and to her surprise, they were standing inside the dark museum. She counted her fingers, all ten, but the ruby ring was gone.

"Did you feel that?" he asked with a sly smile

on his face.

"I feel light as a feather."

"Congratulations. You have now entered another realm. It's called The Veil. You may think it's an acid trip, but we're actually in our spirit forms. Our lifeless bodies are now lying outside the front doors."

Her ring was there, still on her finger. "How...?"

"When you enter The Veil, your soul leaves your body. When you enter any other realm, your body dematerializes and reforms. Any questions?"

"You're not going to tell me how this is possible, are you?"

"Things happen. Things are what they are. The answers to your questions will be completely unimportant once you accept these things."

"I guess I have to trust you."

Evander's facial expression changed from mischievous to gentle. "A little late for that, don't you think?"

He guided her through the museum, as if knowing exactly where to find Rowan. Willow was not frightened in The Veil, however, the thought of her body lying lifeless on the concrete outside unsettled her stomach. She pushed back her feelings of uneasiness and took a look at everything around her. She noticed that her surroundings seemed pristine, like the walls and the paintings were young, innocent children. It was funny to her how purity was discomforting and off-putting. Maybe because she knew the physical world was so corrupt, and she had never known or experienced anything close to true peace. She didn't even know it was possible. She didn't know a lot of things were possible before Evander came around.

When he reached the room Rowan was in, Willow was absolutely enthralled by Rowan's stunning beauty. Her skin looked smooth. Willow had always wanted her hair the shade of Rowan's, a deep feisty and fiery red. Her eyes were mossy green, the kind of green found in pictures of jungles and forests. Willow felt a bit jealous of Rowan. Not that Willow would consider herself unattractive. She thought that she was quite good looking, though physical appearance wasn't her best attribute.

Rowan was in a room that showcased abstract paintings, which were quite colorful. A painter's easel supporting a canvas stood directly in front of her. She balanced a clean wooden paint palette on her right hand while her left hand held a brush. Rowan dipped the brush into nothing at all and began stroking the canvas with it, the bristles leaving no sign of paint or any other substance behind.

"You may want to put down that brush before you injure someone," Evander said as he walked closer to Rowan.

Without turning, she giggled and shook her head. "You know me better than that. I wouldn't hurt a fly." Her voice was one of the joyous voices Willow had ever heard; it was deep and smooth, like a song lay in her throat, on the edge of slipping right out. Willow understood that Evander knew some pretty interesting people, ergo, earth bound spirits, also known as flesh occupied by energy.

He signaled Willow to introduce herself, but Willow couldn't cough up a single word. She thought she was having an anxiety attack, but really, she was experiencing a symptom of transport hangover. According to Evander, traveling to a different realm sometimes caused the traveler to feel various discomforts like headaches, nausea, loss of speech, heart palpitations, bladder infections etc. Transporting wasn't an easy experience for someone who had never done it before.

"Evander, you're an idiot." Rowan's cheeks

were almost as red as her hair.

He actually looked intimidated for a mere second before he rolled his eyes. "I'm not an idiot. Inconsiderate, okay, but an idiot? No."

"If I'd known she'd never transported... Gosh, you really get my motor running, and not in a good way."

"At least it's running."

Rowan scowled at Evander, her brow forming a perfect frown, her eyes screaming with disapproval, almost as if she were Evander's mother giving him a silent lecture for sneaking out of the house on a school night.

As hard as Evander tried to show he was unaffected by Rowan's figurative daggers, his gulping and deep breaths were proof that he took Rowan seriously. "Do you have any more information on the murders?"

Rowan's attitude shifted, her eyes softened as she sighed at the change of topic. "Not anything good. Hattie is no longer with us. I recognized the necklace the killer left at the scene, the garnet stone in a pile of ashes."

Evander clenched his jaw and rubbed at his temples in circular motions. "We've been around for a very long time, and nothing of this nature has ever happened until now. When did peace become such a foreign virtue in our community?"

"That's the sad thing about life, isn't it? Nothing is guaranteed to last forever. Especially peace."

"Last time I checked," Willow chimed in with more volume than expected, seemingly due to her transport hangover, "the world has never been at peace. There's always a war or a conflict or an environmental crisis."

Rowan looked at Willow with pity. "We aren't talking about the earth-world. We're talking about *our* community." She motioned at the space between her and Evander. "We've lived in tranquility for centuries. Though neither Evander nor I have been around since the beginning, we are still very much affected by this...phenomenon. We may be targets, our friends may be targets, heck, our friends *have* been targets."

"Willow is part of this community now too, Rowan. Don't forget that. She is in as much danger as you and I." Evander looked down at his shoes like a shy little boy who was apologizing to his teacher for stealing another student's crayons.

Willow wanted to know why Rowan seemed to be Evander's weak spot, why he was a softer and a more respecting person in her presence. She had something hanging over his head, like an anvil waiting to drop.

"Maybe you shouldn't have dragged her into this mess. We don't need to be responsible for her life."

Evander laughed breathily, but before he could explain the reasons behind his actions toward, and for, Willow, Willow felt the need to defend and prove herself to Rowan.

"Neither of you are responsible for my life. I'm the one who makes the final decision about whether or not to be involved. I *want* to continue training. I want to help you find out who's committing the murders."

Evander and Rowan stared at her like she'd said something wrong.

"I want to be part of something special." She wanted to *be* someone special. Living a normal life was impossible now that she knew there was something for her to discover here, something bigger than herself, something to make her life exciting. "I'm willing to do anything to keep you from kicking me to the curb."

"We could use her as bait," Evander joked.

Rowan wasn't on board with that plan, whether it was a joke or not. "We're looking for a killer. Not a fish."

Chapter 3
TEARS FOR 1968

Evander grew concerned about his and Willow's bodies lying directly outside the museum where any security guard could stumble upon them. After Rowan agreed with Evander about allowing Willow to embark on their journey to find a psycho killer, he decided it would be best to take Willow home. There were a lot of things to discuss, and Willow still had to go through her training. Priorities needed to be established. Some rules needed following, and Evander strongly hoped Willow would be willing to comply. She had a very strong personality. He wasn't sure which box to put her in, or if she would fit into a box in the first place. The further modern times progressed, the larger Looscents' personalities became.

Willow was looking out the car window when Evander cleared his throat and asked her something that couldn't have caught her more off guard.

"How do you know Zander?"

Willow crinkled her nose, "Zan? I've known him for years."

"That doesn't answer my question."

"He works at Crossroads, and I've been going there for years. You know, the coffee shop you followed me to."

He groaned. "Do you consider him a friend?"

"I'm starting to consider *you* a friend. So yes, I consider someone I've known for years a friend. Why are you asking? Do *you* know him?"

Evander shrugged, his eyes focused on the road in front of him. Both hands gripped the steering wheel. "We try to keep our distance. Pretend as though we've never met when we *do* run into each other. It's the best way to go with the condition our relationship is in right now."

"He told me he didn't know you."

"Figures."

Willow murmured to herself. She hated to be surprised with questions asked directly out of the blue. Inquiries of that nature made her want to scream until she was dead, lying in a purple velvet-lined coffin buried deep in the ground. And even then, in the afterlife, she would still be haunted by those peculiar questions.

As Evander made a left turn on the street that led to her home, she began to feel antsy. She wasn't ready to face such familiar territory just yet. She had been waiting for any level of excitement to hit her. Car rides and small talk weren't enough to feed her insatiable craving for precarious escapades. Her neighborhood was dull and smelled of wet dirt, like her childhood did. She'd play in the rain, twirl in a circle, feel the droplets of water land softly on her face. She'd get on her knees and stroke the wet grass, brushing it with her fingers as if she were brushing a person's hair. *The earth needs love too,* she'd think, *the earth should feel loved.* Those were the days when she didn't find crooked picture frames or unorganized medicine cabinets irksome.

"I don't want to go home," she blurted out.

He loosened his grip on the steering wheel and pulled over. "Where would you like to go?" He asked this question the way a taxi driver would sound.

"Anywhere but home." Willow hoped Evander would take her back to his place, where he would serve her tea and talk her ears off. But then she quickly became concerned that Dr. Everly might be there, as well, and Willow wasn't in the mood to listen to more bickering.

They ended up going to a small donut shop just outside the downtown area. A young Armenian man with slicked-back black hair and a well-groomed beard sat on a foldable metal chair behind the counter, reading a newspaper. When they walked in, he didn't look at them right away, instead he just kept reading, his eyes darting from word to word, his lips moving just slightly.

Evander cleared his throat. "I'd like to order."

"Yes," the Armenian man said, barely even acknowledging the fact that they were standing a mere five feet away from him.

Evander squinted and slung his arm protectively over Willow's shoulder. "We'll take two glazed donuts, please."

"Of course." The man folded up his newspaper and rose from the chair. He grabbed two donuts with waxed tissue paper and dropped them into a white bag, then slid it across the counter for Evander to take.

"Well? How much do I owe you?"

The man waved his hand and sat back down. "No."

"Do I not owe you anything?"

"Yes."

Willow guided Evander to a table in the far

corner of the shop. For a few minutes, they ate their donuts in silence, occasionally looking up to smile at each other as if smiling was a way to commence conversation.

Willow spoke first. "Tell me what you know about Zan."

Evander wiped his mouth with a napkin and folded it three times before responding. "What could I possibly tell you that you don't already know?"

"I bet there's plenty I don't know about him."

Evander let out a soft sigh and leaned forward in his seat. He folded his hands on the table and looked at her with doleful eyes. "I don't want to scare you away from him. Or make you resent him."

"I could never."

Evander cleared his throat. "I first met Zander in Italy, I believe it was the day Antonio Lotti passed away, but I can't say for certain. Memories start to get a little fuzzy after a while. The details of our meeting aren't as interesting as I would've liked them, but we grew to be close friends. Unfortunately, I passed away very young. We didn't have much time together. Maybe a year or two."

Willow swallowed. "You're going to have to

clarify a few things for me."

"I will when I'm finished. May I continue?" When Willow nodded her head, he cracked his knuckles as a way to prepare himself to go on with telling his story. "I was reincarnated a few times before meeting *Zan* in the flesh again, though I never spent a life without being reminded of him somehow. When 1922 rolled around, I was eighteen years old and living in New York City. It was a good year, actually one of my favorites for many reasons. Zan was one of those reasons. An old schoolmate invited me to a party at their home. I was hesitant to go at first, but of course, I went. I took one step inside the house and felt Zan's energy magnetize me toward him. It was destiny that I would meet him there, for the first time in a little less than 200 years. I can't recall another time I felt so light."

"He never told me he was over 200 years old." She ground her molars and continued listening.

"We spent the rest of that life together. For the most part, we were inseparable. The connection we had was something special...and then it all ended. I was dying, cancer, you know how that can be. He was sitting next to me on this stupid rocking chair that I deeply wish he'd never bought. It was so damn squeaky." Evander swallowed a bite of his donut. "He told me that he wasn't going to weep for me, because he would see me in another life. I told him he wouldn't. I couldn't bear losing him again, leaving him to go on without me, with someone else. I pushed him away and allowed that feeling to take control of me until my very last moment."

"I can imagine how angry he was." It took everything Willow had to keep herself together. She couldn't believe what she was hearing about the friend she thought she knew so well.

"He was furious. He rose from his chair and started yelling. I'd never seen him out of control, and it was terrifying. The minute I told him I never wanted to let myself get close to him again, I knew it was a mistake. I made a mistake."

"Have you tried apologizing?"

"I made him promise me that if we ever ran into each other again, we would pretend like we'd never met. How does someone apologize for that hurt, that betrayal?"

"You can try."

"I felt his energy around you, Willow, when I first met you. And I bet he felt me on you, as well. I wanted to throw myself into the void, but knowing I was destined to be your spirit guide, I had to ignore his presence in this life."

"That's a little harsh."

"Maybe, but it's true."

***

Evander didn't feel up to talking more about his time with Zan, so he dropped Willow off at her house. She didn't speak to him much on the way, which was expected after he delivered the news that Zan had been hiding so much from her. Instead of heading toward his own apartment, he headed toward Zan's house. He felt no shame in knowing exactly where Zan lived. Evander had wanted to know Zan was safe, so Evander had tracked him down. He never stopped thinking about Zan, and he was confident that Zan never stopped either. A connection like theirs was impossible to break. Almost as impossible to break as the connection between a Looscent and her guide.

All the lights in Zan's house were off and the curtains were closed. Evander should've felt intrusive, just sitting in his car, staring at the small house, but he didn't. The crickets chirping loudly convinced him to walk up those steps, knock on that door, and face the person he let slip right out from under him. He let the stars give him the courage he needed. He let the moonlight illuminate his path. Evander was ready for whatever fate decided to throw at him.

He rang the doorbell twice, knocked twice, and then stood waiting as patiently as possible. He saw lights inside flicker on and a figure pass by the window to the left of the front door. When Zan opened the door, he was absolutely clueless as to why Evander stood directly in front of him.

"What are you doing here?"

"She knows. I told Willow everything. Well, not everything, but some things."

"Oh, wow." Zan shook his head, thinking that it was too late at night to engage in an argument with Evander. "Who made you king of everything? Who made you think you can call every shot and make every decision? Who gave you that right?"

"Can I come in?"

"No, you can't come in. You have the audacity to show up at my house this late, uninvited, to tell me that you exposed me to my best friend. Yet you still expect me to let you inside? Where does your mind go when you do these things?"

Evander stepped forward and laid both his hands on Zander's shoulders. "Please let me inside."

Zan huffed and shrugged his shoulders to get

Evander's hands off. Knowing he wouldn't take no for an answer, Zan turned his back to Evander and walked inside the house.

Evander trailed behind him and shut the door. He stared at Zan's tense back, waiting for any sudden movement, waiting for the right moment to say sorry or to say anything at all.

Zan took a seat on his sofa.

Evander did the same. "Have you heard about the murders?" Evander figured death would be a safe topic of conversation to start with.

"Of course. You and Rowan must be scrambling."

"We are. She misses you. We both do."

Zan huffed again, not wanting to give into Evander's sudden warm-heartedness. "Why are you here? Haven't you done enough?"

"I know I should be here. I should've always been here."

"Should've, would've, could've, but you weren't."

"That can change. We could start off slow. Just be civil with each other. I need you, you know. I need you to be safe. If you were *killed* and I knew I could've done something to prevent that, I would never be able to live with myself."

"Who have we become? I thought you hated

the idea of star-crossed lovers losing each other again."

Evander laughed. His nerves eased, hearing Zan make light of their past loving relationship.

Zan leaned his head back and stared upwards at nothing in particular. He just wanted to look away from the person next to him, refuse to give in to whatever Evander was planning in that messy head of his.

Zan's hands were folded in his lap, like Willow's often were. He appeared to be much more grown up and mature, compared to the last time Evander saw him. Taking in his current human form, Evander's mind raced through memories of them together. Times they traveled, times they shared dinner plates, times they stayed up past four a.m., talking about how insignificant they felt living on earth. Evander wasn't kidding when he'd told Willow they were once inseparable. Evander hated being separated from Zan, even if just for a few minutes. They were unhealthily codependent, but it worked for them. It *used to* work for them. Evander scooted a few inches closer to Zan. "Thank you for forgiving me."

"I never said I forgive you. I'm tolerating you."

"What will make you forgive me? A box of

imported chocolates?"

Zan wearily groaned. "I don't want Willow to get hurt. She has a lot of spiritual skills to learn. She's just a beginner."

"You underestimate her."

"I love her as much as I love you." Zan momentarily let his guard down for the sake of satisfying Evander, even though nothing would ever satisfy him. Evander was an exhausting person to be around. Zan just wanted to get their talk over with.

Evander's insides twisted and turned a few dozen times before he properly processed Zan's blatant declaration of love, whether he actually meant it or not. "I'm quite fond of you," Evander said softly.

Nothing would ever be the same between them, and they both knew it. But in some interesting way, it was for the better that things changed. Change wasn't always preferred, but sometimes it was absolutely necessary. Zan had to know that it would've been impossible to stay away from each other until the day the sun decided not to rise. A lot of things he said to Evander were said out of anger and the hurt of rejection, but that didn't mean what he said wasn't valid or justified. He had called Evander every bad name in the book, even when he knew Evander was dying and in pain. Seems the insults hurt less with every life lived, even when spoken by someone Evander thought had loved him.

Chapter 4
LET'S PLAY FORGIVENESS

Willow set her mind on one mission, to scold Zan for being secretive, a liar, and a poor excuse for a friend. She needed an honest explanation as to why he hid such a huge part of himself and his life from her, especially considering she was supposed to be high up on the spiritual food-chain. There was simply so much she didn't know, and not even her one friend, her best friend, had been honest with her. She understood that being in his position must've been tough, but he had to know that the chances of her finding out about him were very high.

She slipped into the first pair of jeans she could find and threw on an old sweatshirt she found on the floor in the corner of her closet. She didn't bother brushing her hair or putting on socks, risking a blister just to save time. There was nothing more she wanted to do than yell at Zan.

She was enraged when people lied to her, which made her feel like a hypocrite, because she was also telling lies of her own.

The walk to Zan's house wasn't particularly long, so taking a bus or calling a cab wasn't necessary. The morning weather was gloomy and appropriate for mourning the death of a close family member or friend. Orange and yellow leaves scattered across the narrow neighborhood streets. Even with the pop of colors around her, she couldn't find anything positive about her day or the circumstances she faced.

She inhaled many deep breaths before knocking on Zan's door. As she waited for him to answer, she thought about what her first words to him would be. Before she had much time to think, Zan opened the door. "Well, this is unexpected."

"Did you feel good about lying to me? Or was it eating you alive? I hope it was eating you alive."

"Lied? I've never *lied* to you."

"Not telling me the truth about Evander was a lie. You told me you never met the guy. You could've given me some kind of a warning. You've known the whole time, haven't you? You've known about me being this...this spirit *thing*. And you're an immortal...*something*."

Zan sighed in shame. "You're a Looscent. I'm

an Idio."

"All this time I thought you were a friend. I thought I could always count on you."

Zan gulped and dropped his shoulders. He didn't like her yelling at him. He often complained that her high pitched voice hurt his eardrums.

"What do you want me to say? If admit that I lied, you're just going to get angrier. If I don't, you're just going to get angrier. Either way, you're angry and I'm a jerk."

"Damn right you are."

"And I deserve everything you have to say to me."

"Damn right you do."

"But I'm still the same person. Nothing has changed. So, you can either turn around and leave here angry, or you can stay and let me answer whatever questions you may have."

She chose the latter. A fire burned inside her and she clung to a thin string of hope that Zan's explanation would be enough to put out that blaze.

"He was here last night. I had the feeling he was gonna get on his knees and beg if I didn't give him what he wanted. That would've been embarrassing for both of us." Zan led her into his kitchen where he prepared a fresh pot of coffee.

Coffee always helped her relax. Caffeine affected her in strange ways.

She crossed her arms, only guarding herself from Zan's willingness to do whatever it took to keep her from hating him. "What did he want?"

Zan shrugged. "Forgiveness."

"And you forgave him?"

"To him, he's forgiven." Zan leaned against the counter and cocked his head to the side. "But I still hold a grudge against him for telling me he never wanted to see me again."

"So, you're playing mind games."

Zan snapped his fingers and pointed at her as if they weren't engaged in a serious conversation. "You're thinking in the right direction." He slapped his thigh. "This situation that we're all in, with the murders, you and Evander meeting, my past with Evander...it's something I never thought would land in my lap. Your safety and well-being are important beyond words. So, if keeping you safe and not jeopardizing your training with Evander requires me to get along with him, then you better believe that's what I'll do. I'd hate for you to be thrown out of this world all because I couldn't stow my chick-flick-like antipathy towards a *guy*."

"So now what? You, Evander, and I are all

gonna try to live in perfect harmony with each other when you really want to kick him to the curb and leave him in the gutter?"

Zan looked to the ceiling then back at her. "Pretty much."

She rolled her eyes and opened one of Zan's overhead cabinets to grab a mug. She happened to get the one with a picture of a willow tree on it that she had given Zan as a Christmas gift. He'd gone through a phase of constantly reminding her and making jokes about her being named after a tree, of all things, so she bought him a mug to commemorate that time. They were an odd pair.

"Evander keeps saying he needs to train me, but we never go anywhere or get anything done. I feel like he's pulling my strings."

Zan took the mug from her hand a filled it with coffee. "Training is a long process. I think he's just feeling things out with you. You're scary sometimes."

She thrust her shoulders back and smiled. "Good."

The two friends sat on Zan's front porch steps, drinking their coffees and sharing a kind of silence only they were able to enjoy together. The clouds started to clear, letting the sun heat them up. She hadn't expected to feel relieved of stress. Her mind was at ease, at least until a very recognizable crow landed in front of her, almost making both her and Zan spill their coffees.

"Can't you leave me alone for just a day?" Willow slammed her mug down on the concrete step and leaned forward. "How do you always know where I am?"

Zan stared at her, wide-eyed. "What are you doing?"

She scowled at the bird. "She's Evander's friend, Dr. Everly."

Zan directed his attention to the crow–form of Dr. Everly as she flapped her wings and jumped up and down. "I think she wants you to follow her."

Reluctantly, Willow bid Zan farewell. She followed the bird for about two miles before stopping in front of a four-story abandoned warehouse not far from Evander's apartment. Not knowing what she was meant to do there, she turned around and noticed that Dr. Everly had already flown off, leaving her on her own.

She looked up at the windows that reckless imbeciles had broken out with rocks. Colorful and fading graffiti covered a large portion of the lower half of the building. The warehouse was decaying, but Willow felt an overwhelming sense of purpose coming from it. She then heard someone yell from one of the broken windows, and she followed the voice until she saw Evander waving frantically from the fourth story.

"I'll come get you. Wait there," he yelled.

Moments later, a grey metal door set off to her left opened, and without even saying hello to Evander, she complained, "How does Dr. Everly always know where I am?"

Evander shook his head. "Where were you?"

"I was at Zan's this morning. He told me you were there last night."

Evander smirked slyly at her and waved his arm toward the door. "You wanna come in or not?"

He guided her through the warehouse in the same way he had guided her through the museum. They passed by many rooms filled with copious amounts of dust and rubble. Some pieces of the ceiling had fallen down, and many walls had gaping holes, as if someone had taken a sledgehammer to them. Even with the cobwebs and the occasional rat squealing across the floor, the way the building seemed frozen in time appealed to her.

"Rowan is in here," Evander said as he took a sharp turn into a room with three windows on one wall, all draped with peach see-through curtains. A few mismatched vintage chairs were placed in a circle in the center of the room. Rowan sat comfortably on one of them with her tan legs crossed while she examined her fingernails. The room wasn't as dilapidated as others. It looked as if Evander, Rowan, or someone else had cleaned it up at one time.

As Willow stepped through the doorframe, a little golden bell rang overhead. "That's happened before. That bell. What does it mean?"

Rowan rose from her chair. "It happens when any Idio or Omni step into a room occupied by other Idios or Omni, whom they haven't physically met before their moment of clarity. Evander, have you told her nothing? Nothing at all?"

Evander rolled his eyes. "What I do and don't tell her is none of your business, *dear*."

Rowan pursed her lips. "Willow, do you even have a clue about what you're doing here?"

She shifted her body weight. "No. But I bet Evander was just about to explain, right?" She didn't know whose team to side with but figured it might be best to stay on Evander's, though it didn't hurt to make fun of him when the opportunity arose.

Evander turned his back to her and took a seat on one of the chairs, landing with a thump. "You're here because I'm gonna teach you how to transport. It's the easiest step in training, and I think you might master it today if you try hard enough."

"Transport where?"

"You can transport to different realms, or transport to a different time period. You've already transported twice before, but it was with my help. You need to learn to do it on your own."

"What are we gonna work on first?"

Evander looked up to the water-damaged ceiling. "I'm in the mood for time travel. Do you have an item with you that's older than you?"

"This whole building is older than me."

"No. A single *object*. Something you're familiar with."

She looked down at her right hand. When she was about twelve, her mother gave her a ring with an oval ruby. It was the ring Willow's dad had used when he proposed to Elizabeth back in April of 1995. He asked her to marry him after a concert in Chicago on a cold Friday night. Willow didn't purposely wear the ring all the time, but she never had a reason to take it off, other than when washing dishes, sleeping, or going through airport security.

She held her hand up in front of Evander's face. "Will my mom's engagement ring work?"

He slipped the ring off of her finger. "Perfectly."

Evander went on to explain how every object had a life. How times and places could be locked into something inanimate, just waiting to be discovered and explored.

Willow listened intently to every word he said, hoping to grasp the information properly. The concept of objects possessing spiritual qualities intrigued her. She was excited to master the skill of time travel, so she could dig through boxes of old memorabilia and go back to each of their times.

"You have to become one with the ring," Evander said with his pointer finger wiggling in the air.

"Am I gonna turn into a cave dwelling creature?" Willow scoffed.

Evander didn't understand that pop-culture reference. He didn't seem like the type who kept up with the latest superhero movies or newly released books. But she appreciated his dry sense of humor. She realized how quickly she had warmed up to him.

Evander directed her to sit cross-legged with him on the floor. Her nose tickled from all of the dust in the air. It didn't seem to bother Evander or Rowan.

Rowan slowly paced back and forth. Her high heels clicking on the floor sounded like a metronome.

Evander's hair was a mess. His curls rested gently against his clammy forehead and dangled down across his eyes. His jeans had two holes in them, one on each knee, and he wore a necklace, a black wire-wrapped tourmaline spear, that hung loosely around his neck. He placed the ring in front of him on the floor and stretched out both his hands for Willow to take. "Close your eyes and create a vision of the ring in your mind. Once you've got it, I'm going let go."

Willow nodded and closed her eyes. She cleared her mind of anything but her mother's ruby ring, picturing every scratch on the band and the way the stone shimmered in bright light. After a few seconds of extreme concentration, she heard noises that couldn't possibly be coming from outside the warehouse. She heard cars honking and people talking, some louder than others. Then she felt her body get hot. Droplets of sweat collected at the back of her neck. She couldn't feel

Evander's hands anymore, so she opened her eyes and found herself sitting at an outdoor café. Evander sat across from her, sipping iced tea.

"Where are we?" she asked while frantically looking around.

"I have no idea. Do you see the ring anywhere?"

Willow looked at her hand, no ring, then glanced at everyone's fingers, hoping to find someone wearing the ring. She was about to say no when she spotted a woman who looked like a younger version of her mom, sitting alone at a table, twisting a ring on the ring finger of her left hand.

"My mom is wearing it."

Evander snorted. "Of course she is. It was her ring, wasn't it?"

"What year is this?"

He looked down at his left wrist, as if looking at a watch to check the time. "It's June of 1996. And we're currently taking the places of a man and a woman by the names of Robert and Debby. In 1996, at this time, Robert and Debby were sitting right where we're sitting."

"I feel nauseous."

"You'll get over it. Let's walk and talk."

Evander stood up from his seat and patted her

shoulder. She followed him as he walked around, looking intrusively at people's drinks and food.

"Can anybody see us?"

"Nope. We can poke and pry as much as we want, and nothing will alter any event in the future. Look," Evader pointed, "someone's approaching your mom. I think it's a waitress."

Willow trailed Evander as he walked toward Elizabeth. As they reached her table, her conversation with the waitress became clear.

"Beautiful ring," the waitress said as she poured more iced lemon water into Elizabeth's glass. "Where did you get it?"

She had a wistful look in her eyes. "My fiancé—"

"You're getting married." The waitress squealed. "When's the wedding? I mean, I don't mean to be nosy. I'm a sucker for romance."

"We're not...there's no wedding, actually."

The waitress's smile quickly turned into a frown. "I'm sorry."

Elizabeth wiped a tear from her cheek with her dainty fingers. "Oh, it's all right. It wouldn't have worked. We're two opposites, you know? We fight all the time. I wanted to settle down and he wanted to travel. I wanted children and he wanted a dog. Anyway, we wouldn't have been happy together."

The waitress said, "I guess nothing last forever."

"I've loved him for a long time. And I always will."

"Maybe you two can find a way to make it work. You can't give up that easily, miss. You love him? You go get him."

Elizabeth's eyes watered, and she gave the waitress a smile. "Maybe you're right. How bad can it be to own a dog?"

Willow felt more nauseous than before. Her mother never told her about her father leaving. Hearing her mother speak with such longing made her want to cry.

Evander pulled her toward him and hugged her tight. In this out-of-the-ordinary event, she allowed Evander to hold her, and she wrapped her arms securely around his waist. "My parents found a way to make it work."

"Proves opposites attract."

"I just wish they wouldn't fight so much."

"Would you like to go back to our time?" he mumbled into her hair.

She nodded and let Evander do the work to get back to the warehouse. When she woke up, she was lying on the floor. Her head was in Evander's lap, and he was stroking the side of her face.

"Maybe you should channel a different emotion next time," he said.

She furrowed her brows and locked eyes with him. "You didn't warn me about channeling emotions." Her throat felt scratchy.

"I may have forgotten that detail."

"Take me home."

On the way to her house, he told her about transporting and traveling, though she was far too tired to pay much attention. He quieted down after he saw her rest her head against the window.

She hated feeling sad. She didn't want a black cloud hovering over her head or thousand-pound weights on her shoulders. She didn't enjoy feeling like time wasn't passing quickly enough, or even worse, like time was passing far too quickly. Sadness was hard to get over. She could burst into tears at any given moment.

"We're pulling up to your house. Any last words?" Evander asked, as if hoping to make her crack a smile.

"My mother's outside."

Elizabeth was watering plants in the front yard.

Evander parked alongside the curb.

Elizabeth quickly took notice of the car, and as

soon as she saw Willow open the passenger door to get out, her expression turned to anger.

Willow took a few steps up the driveway, and then Evander drove off, leaving her and her mother to themselves.

Elizabeth tossed aside the water hose. "Where have you been all day?"

"Nowhere," she said in the mousiest voice possible. After all, who would believe she went to 1996?

"Who brought you home? That wasn't Zan's car. What have I told you about taking rides from strangers?"

"He isn't a stranger, he's a friend. It's fine. I'm home now."

She walked quickly past her mother and headed for her bedroom. She could hear her mother yelling after her, but all she wanted to do was throw herself on her bed and sulk.

She skipped dinner that evening. Thankfully she had a leftover slice of pizza.

Chapter 5
DESPERATE CALLS

Willow had a perfect night's sleep, so she should've felt ready to start her day. Instead, she felt the complete opposite. After dragging her body into the shower, she hoped cold water would help her feel better. It didn't.

When she went downstairs, her mother didn't speak to her. Elizabeth was still sore about their interaction after Evander dropped her off. She felt bad for being so vague with her mother. She felt bad about the lies. Not knowing what to say made her miserable. She had a strong urge to tell her mom what she had heard back at the café, but she couldn't because there was absolutely no possible way she could explain how she'd found out about their separation when they were engaged. Elizabeth would've forced her to talk about things she would much rather keep secret.

Today was the day her mother had made an

appointment for Willow to see Dr. Everly. No music played on the drive to the office. They didn't speak to each other.

Willow, once again, found herself sitting in Dr. Everly's always-creepy waiting room. Elizabeth sat silently next to her, reading a celebrity gossip magazine. Willow prayed for Evander to arrive with his usual confidence, and sure enough, her prayers were answered. The door to the office flung open.

Evander sauntered in with his hands in his pockets. He'd combed his hair straight back and styled it with too much hairspray.

"Good morning, ladies," he said, a little flirtatiously.

Willow offered him a smile and he winked at her in return.

"Good morning," Elizabeth said, barely glancing up from her magazine.

After he sat down, Evander and Willow continued to stare at each other. He gave her a sorrowful look as a way to apologize for the situation without using words.

Willow responded by rolling her eyes.

Evander coughed into his fist, which made Elizabeth tear her eyes away from her reading material and stare at him.

"Ma'am." He dipped his chin.

"You look familiar, young man." She spoke with a softness Willow wasn't used to.

"We've met. My name is Evander."

"Oh, right. I remember you. Are you waiting for your appointment too?"

"Not exactly. I'm here for your *daughter's* appointment."

Willow scowled at him.

Her mother's jaw slacked, yet she recovered quickly as if no longer fazed by his remark. "May I ask why?"

He shrugged. "I'm shadowing Eira. I hope to learn from her by watching the way she works."

"Well, aren't you charming," Willow whispered, earning an evil glare from her mother.

"That's very good. It's nice to meet young people who have goals set for their lives." A sideways glance told Willow she wasn't included in those young people.

Dr. Everly had perfect timing. She opened her office door and beckoned Willow to go inside. Evander followed her in, and after sending one last smile Elizabeth's way, he shut the door behind him.

She thought there was a rule against psychologists sharing patient's information with other people for the sake of the patient's privacy. If that rule was in place, her mother didn't seem to care much about it.

"What was that all about?" Willow snarled.

Evander laughed deeply, probably loud enough for her mother to hear. "I have everything under control. Do you really think I'm charming?"

Willow hit him hard in his shoulder, knocking him back a bit, and then noticed Dr. Everly speaking to a dark-skinned man with silver hair and perfectly symmetrical features. He was covered in tattoos, from what Willow was able to tell from his wrists and neck. The man was wearing a black trench coat; it was un-buttoned, revealing a pleated white dress shirt. Black suspenders held up his pants. There were three scars on his right temple, which could've easily been mistaken for white ink tattoos.

When the room went silent, Dr. Everly introduced the man to Willow. "This is Ebra."

Evander didn't look pleased to be in the same room as Ebra. He straightened out his back and bit his bottom lip so hard that Willow thought he would draw blood.

"I've heard plenty about you, Willow." Ebra shook her hand. His voice was smooth and soulful, stupendously daunting.

"I'm sorry to say that I've heard nothing about you, sir," she said, not looking at his face.

"Eira, a word," Evander commanded and pulled her to the back of the room.

***

Evander didn't appreciate being surprised with the presence of someone he strongly disliked and disapproved of. "Why is he here?" he asked, not afraid to hold back his displeasure.

Eira wouldn't take any snark from Evander, even if her life depended on it. "I don't have to explain myself to you."

"He's manipulative and deceitful, and I would prefer he stay far away from Willow."

Dr. Everly's stare could've burned holes in Evander's soul. "Ebra has information about the murders."

"It better be helpful."

Eira clenched her jaw and stomped her delicate heel. "No more of this nonsense." She walked away, leaving Evander to bask in his anger.

She's doing it again, falling for the con's allure and leaving everything else behind.

She had done that before. Evander knew her patterns. Eira was so weak and desperate for attention, that she couldn't help but throw herself at Ebra.

Everyone had a personal choice of poison, whether it was desire for riches, alcohol, or mendacious men who had a knack for using people, taking away their purity, and then throwing them away like the daily trash. Ebra was the last person Evander would ever go to for help, because Ebra only had his own best interests in mind. Eira was too dense to see that for herself, no matter how much Evander tried to turn her against Ebra.

***

Willow was in a daze, listening to Ebra. He rambled on about switchblades and Swiss army knives. She didn't know one man could know so much about daggers and swords. He was spooky. When Eira wrapped her dainty hand around Ebra's bicep and began speaking in a dispirited manner, Willow broke out of her daze.

"Ebra, darling," Eira said. "We'll have to continue this conversation another time." Dr. Everly looked up at him like he was the sun and she was a flower growing toward the light. Her alabaster skin glowed when she was near him.

"Understandable." Ebra placed his hand on top of Eira's, and in the blink of an eye, he was gone.

Eira was left standing with her hand in midair. She didn't say much for the rest of Willow's appointment. She sat on her chair, quietly staring off into space, occasionally blinking.

Evander paced anxiously, obviously thinking, and Willow had no choice but to alternate between staring at him and staring at Dr. Everly. The office was chilly, and Willow didn't have a jacket. Nobody seemed to notice her teeth chattering or her full-body shivers.

"Maybe we should work on training," Willow said, shifting her gaze to the vacuumed carpet.

Evander stopped in his tracks but completely ignored Willow. "Eira, what did Ebra tell you about the murders?"

She avoided looking directly at him. "Their bodies are being lit on fire. When the spirit detaches itself from its vessel, it is then captured and hidden in a different realm."

"How did he obtain this knowledge?"

"I just listen and don't ask questions."

"You question every person but him. Why do you trust him? And don't tell me you love him."

"Love is nothing without trust," Eira growled.

He huffed. "I'm taking Willow elsewhere. This environment is toxic."

Evander placed his hand on the back of Willow's neck as if he was going to choke her. She flinched when his cold fingers came in contact with her chilled skin. Then she felt a rough push, like Evander used all the strength in his body to push her body down and forward. In a millisecond, he had transported her and himself to the shack on the beach, with the piano, from her dreams. She didn't appreciate him just flicking her into a different realm without letting her know first.

She tore herself from his grasp and spun around to face him. He had a murderous look in his eyes.

"What's going on with you and Dr. Everly? And who in god's name is Ebra?" she asked, watching Evander's body stand perfectly still.

"Eira is a fool. She's an aggressive fool who is in absolute denial."

"She and Ebra, they're together...like a couple?"

"She's devoted herself to him. I would rather she devote herself to Typhon, the Father of Monsters. Ebra consumes her entire being. He's a leech."

"How do you think he knows so much about the murders?"

Evander turned his back to her and took a seat on the piano bench. He dropped his head and played a single chord, making the muscles in his back move noticeably under the thin shirt he was wearing. "I can't say for sure."

Willow noticed him trying to hide his worry. She sat next to him and gave his shoulders a light rub. She was growing fond of him. It pained her to see him in distress, even if it was mild. She listened to him play melancholy songs and hum along to the melodies he created. She had been through enough to know that patience was one of the most important virtues anyone could have. And she didn't want to be just his student. He tried hard to make her think he was a mentally stable person, but she knew he wasn't, and she wanted to be there for him. She wanted to be his friend.

Evander hated showing weakness. He took pride in being brave and resilient. But then humanity slapped him across the face, and he realized that being human came with flaws. With flaws came frailty. No human could ever feel as if the universe favored him, or her, every day of the year. At noon on any given day, he might feel okay, which also meant at noon on any given day, he might not feel okay. Evander had trouble accepting that not feeling okay was part of living.

The sun will continue to rise and the earth will continue to rotate, he would tell himself, *at least for another billion years,* and knowing that, he'd feel a little better.

"What are we going to do when we find the killer?" she asked, hoping Evander wouldn't tense up again.

"Find a way to destroy him before he destroys us."

"Us?"

"That's why we have to work on your training and finish as soon as possible. If you die before then, you'll go to a place where defective spirits can never escape."

Willow thought of what step to take next, but before she could ask another question, Evander turned to her. "We should go back and talk to Zan."

***

Evander flash-transported himself and Willow back to Dr. Everly's office, where they found her in the same position they had left her in. She paid no attention to them once they were in her presence again. It was odd to see her in a vegetative state. Willow was used to seeing the psychiatrist responsive and observant. It did truly seem like Ebra had consumed her entire being.

Willow sat on the chair in front of Dr. Everly's desk. "Do you need some water?"

Dr. Everly shook her head. "Do not dare let others tear something good away from you for *their* sake."

Evander slammed his palms down on Dr. Everly's desk. "Eira. For the sake of *us*, I never want Ebra in this room while Willow and I are here. Do with him what you wish, but I will not allow Willow to be near him. I can choose to not include you on all future discussions of the murders, you know. I don't need more problems."

Eira looked toward Willow. "You liked him, didn't you, dear?"

Willow shrugged. "He has a nice coat."

Evander did nothing but mumble to himself for the remainder of Willow's appointment, and Willow had no choice but to listen and sit patiently. When the little timer on Eira's desk rang, she harshly shut it off, and returned to her statuesque position. As Willow exited the office to join her mother in the waiting room, Evander whispered for her to meet him back at Zan's house.

Willow was hesitant to ask her mother to drop

her off at Zan's house. Elizabeth was already growing agitated about Willow being out of the house so often without communicating where she had been or what she had been doing.

"Zan invited me over today," Willow said in a tiny voice.

"Are you implying that you want me to leave you at Zan's house?"

"Just for a few hours. I'm helping him with some stuff."

Her mother sighed deeply and made a left turn on a street called Empire, heading in the direction of Zan's residence.

***

As soon as her mother drove away, Willow rang Zan's doorbell. Seconds later, Evander appeared in the doorway with a big smile on his face. His attitude had shifted for the better. It was as if his presence in the same vicinity as Zan equated to being struck by lightning, electrifying and brightening him up, minus the fire, mass destruction, and eardrum-splitting thunder.

"Hey, stranger," she said, earning an even bigger smile from him. He moved aside to let her in.

She found Zan in the kitchen, his favorite room

in the house, waiting for the water in his teakettle to boil. He wore his white shirt, the one with the coffee stains, and his purple contact lenses. He had a shift at Crossroads later that day.

Evander clapped his hands together unexpectedly. "Zan and I were discussing our encounter with Ebra."

Zan nodded. "He has a dog named Butch. She bit me once."

"How do you know Ebra?" Willow asked.

Evander snorted. "He's everywhere. He's like the plague."

"I bet he uses both armrests at the movie theater," Zan commented.

Willow watched as the two men continued to make witty comebacks about Ebra. Even after Zan stated that Ebra wore too much strong cologne on purpose, Willow still didn't have an actual clue as to why Ebra was so terrible, other than his bizarreness. The first impression he made on her was that he was pretentious, but a lot of people were pretentious, so she didn't immediately assume he was a terrible a person.

She rolled her eyes. "So he's that guy who drinks scotch straight from the bottle. Can either of you explain to me why he's so bad?"

Evander's smile faded slightly, as well as

Zan's. "When I was in your position, Willow, he was my guide, and he put me through hell. It was training every day for hours. I hardly slept, I hardly ate, and a few times, I almost died in the process. As you can imagine, I've known him for a very long time, and he just keeps tracking me down and finding ways to contact me, like he's bound himself to me. I've also known Eira for as long as I've known him."

"He got in between us," Zan interrupted, scratching his arms skittishly.

"He's the one who filled my head with doubt. What he failed to tell me was that I was not obligated to fulfill my duties as a Numinist. I would not be thrown into the pit if I decided to live for myself. That's something important for you to know, Willow. After you've successfully evolved into a Numinist, you can take as much time as you want to decide whether or not you'd like to guide a soul such as yourself."

Willow giggled. "I don't think I'd know how. Can't even guide my own life."

"You'd know how. It would be natural instinct."

The three of them drank tea in Zan's living room. Zan recommended that they forget about Ebra and Eira and anything else that made them feel uneasy. Too much was going on all at once, and stress levels were rising. Willow could sense that the two men were still trying to get reacquainted. They would shoot each other glances and smirks, almost as if they were trying to reassure each other that neither would leave again. When that theory came to Willow's mind, she remembered what Zan had told her about being nice to Evander for safety's sake. Zan was her best friend, but Evander didn't deserve to be tricked or used either. She was unsure of what to think about Zan's out-of-the-ordinary lack of empathy.

Evander broke her out of her musing. "We should work on finding Willow's animal form. Do you still do spell-work, Zan?"

He nodded and put his mug down on the table then got up and ran down his short hallway. Willow wasn't aware Zan did any kind of spell-work or witchcraft. *I learn something new every day.* Zan hadn't revealed much about himself to her, and there was a lot more she'd discover about him.

When Zan came back into the room, he held a red wooden box with intricate engravings of angels and shapes that looked like constellations. He carefully set it down on his coffee table, pulled a bronze key from his pocket, and opened the lock. When he opened the lid, a strong smell of lavender escaped, making Willow gag. She hated lavender.

"What is all this?" she asked, referring to the organized collection of herbs and flowers in individually labeled sheer-white sachets. In the upper left corner rested a smaller box, and a rolled piece of fabric, both of which Zan ignored. In the upper right corner was a deck of what looked like tarot cards held together by a thin white ribbon. Zan pulled them out, untied the ribbon, and began placing each card face-down on the table. By the time he was finished, there were about fifty cards placed evenly apart from each other. He was experienced, not the first time he'd done this. She wanted to ask him if there was a word for a male witch, or if *witch* was the term for both genders.

Zan looked up at Evander and pointed at the floor-to-ceiling bookshelf next to the front door. "Can you get my book of spells? And there's a box under my bed full of candles, can you get that for me too?"

Evander swiftly rose from his seat. He slid out a thick leather-bound book, and with two hands, he handed it to Zan before going to fetch the candles. He came back quickly with a box similar to the one incasing the herbs and put it on the floor next to Zan. He used the same bronze key to unlock it.

"Shall we begin?" Zan sounded like a teacher asking a full classroom if they were ready to begin a lesson.

Evander took a seat next to her. She ended up stuck between him and Zan on the sofa. Zan held her right hand, Evander held her left, and they began to breathe together in a meditative manner. She slipped into a trance and allowed her consciousness to sink into her center.

"Willow, I want you to stick out your hand and let it hover over the table," Evander whispered.

She did as she was told and held her hand over the many cards placed on the table.

"Do you feel like your hand is being nudged in any particular direction?"

She nodded and quietly said, "Yes."

"Good. Let your hand float around until you feel gravity strongly pull it downward."

She hovered for a good two minutes, letting her hand move freely over every card, until it felt as if a magnet was pulling her hand to the table. She figured that was what Evander was talking about when he mentioned a gravitational pull.

"You can open your eyes now," Evander said.

She fluttered her eyes open and immediately noticed her steady hand directly above a single card, unable to move anywhere but down. She looked at Evander, who signaled for her to pick up the card. For a moment she fantasized about what would be under the card.

Would a billion insects crawl out from underneath it?

Would it be blank?

Would she be magically transported to an alternate dimension at first glance?

She took a deep breath and anxiously grabbed the card then flipped it over in the palm of her hand. On the card was a drawing of a woman with the head of a lioness and wearing ancient Egyptian clothing and holding the ankh. On the bottom, in bold lettering, was the name Bastet.

"What does this mean?" she asked.

Evander had a sly smile on his face. "This is Bastet. She's the goddess of cats."

Willow furrowed her eyebrows. "Cats, as in the animal?"

"No, as in the Broadway musical."

Zan sighed heavily about Evander's attempt at making a joke, and then flipped through his spell book until he reached a page covered in handwriting. "We need a white, a black, a grey, a magenta, and a red candle."

"My animal form is also a cat," Evander said, ignoring Zan's statement about candles.

Willow grabbed the five colored candles required and stood them up on the table. "What are we doing next?"

"Performing a blood sacrifice," Zan mumbled sarcastically as he traced his pointer finger along a sentence in his book. Evander grabbed and unrolled the piece of fabric from the box and laid it out on the table, showing the pentagram printed on it.

"We're doing a ritual to invoke the powers of Bastet, for her to supply you the strength and courage to transform efficiently. To do that requires a simple, harmless summoning spell."

"I thought there was only one deity?"

Evander clenched his teeth and tilted his head. "That's where things get tricky. You're correct. There is only one deity. However, these gods and goddesses from various religions and cultures do exist, but they've been understandably mislabeled. Notable figures such as Bastet are Undergods, workers of the true deity."

"Like angels?" Willow placed the colored candles on each point of the pentagram laid out on the table.

"Not exactly angels. Just workers. Think of them like the Higher Power's employees."

Willow folded her hands in her lap, pondering the idea of Undergods.

Zan lit the candles and placed Bastet's tarot card in the center of the pentagram and repositioned himself in order to hold Willow's hand again. Evander did the same.

"Place yourself in ancient Egypt," Zan said in a hushed tone. "Feel the radiating sun on your skin and picture the hot sand extending miles beyond where the eye can see. Visualize yourself tiptoeing through a temple, the only source of light being torches, dimly illuminating your path toward Bastet." A moment of silence passed before he continued. "She is beautiful, she is powerful, and she stares further into you as you approach her. She beckons you to get closer, to tell her what you request from her. Ask for her blessing to transform, ask for her guidance. Allow her into your vessel."

Willow felt heat in her core, like she had just gulped down an entire pot of boiling soup. The warmth felt as loving as the feeling of being hugged by someone she hadn't seen in a long time. She felt her body tense but not uncomfortably. She felt her bones rearrange themselves like puzzle pieces. It was a euphoric experience.

Suddenly, her nails felt longer and much stronger, and when she opened her eyes, her sight was distorted. She saw the room with a much lower saturation, as if viewing it from a very old camera. Everything around her seemed much larger. She didn't remember drinking any shrinking potions. The only possible reason why her perspective on the world had shifted so drastically was because her transformation into a feline had been completed. When she tried to talk, nothing came out, neither words nor a meow. She tried many times but was at a loss.

Without opening his mouth, Evander spoke, and his words were as clear as day in her mind.

"How do you feel?" he asked with a small smile creeping onto his face. His voice echoed in her head.

"I feel strange," she thought back.

Evander erupted in laughter. He reached over to her and stroked her back. The sensation was mesmerizing.

"Don't expect the attention just because you're an animal. You can't go off and have an animal wedding and have animal babies. Other cats will be aware that you're not like them. This form is functional; you can scratch, hiss, and purr as much as a normal cat, but think of this as a demo to a game you aren't able to purchase the full version of yet. You can only do so much."

"Then what's the point of this?" she asked.

"It's fun for the most part, but mostly it's a defense tactic. Cats move quickly and have nine lives."

Excitement pooled in her stomach. She jumped off the sofa, landing on all four paws, and tested out her new form. She crawled under the sofa and was disgusted by how dirty it was underneath. She wondered about the last time Zan used a vacuum cleaner, because the lost and forgotten pieces of food were getting moldy. She scurried out from underneath the sofa and sprinted around the living room, adrenaline running through her veins. She clawed at the rug under Zan's coffee table.

"Stop that," Zan demanded without moving his lips.

Willow jumped up on his lap, accidently digging her nails into his thigh. He winced, petted her head and stroked her back, which started to get a little weird. Before Evander helped her transform back to her normal self, he requested that she occasionally practice shifting on her own time so she could get used to her animal form. She said she would, and within a few short moments, she was sitting back on the couch, furless and clawless.

When Zan took off for his shift at the coffee shop, Evander offered to take Willow home. She thought about it while leaning on the passenger door of his glitzy car. She stared up at the sky. It was that strange time of day when it wasn't noon anymore, but it wasn't late enough to be evening. It was an awkward time, she felt. Mid-afternoon, like the day was already over even though there were many hours left to do something important, and they had many important things to do.

Evander stared at her as she thought about how she wanted to use the last few hours of the day. "Do you want to go to the cemetery?" he asked. "We could read headstones and try to feel alive."

Willow turned her attention to him. "That's morbid," she said with a blank expression, though a smile formed in the back of her mind.

"There's a farm on the outskirts of town. We could chase chickens around."

Willow shook her head at him, thinking he couldn't possibly be serious. "Something's confusing me."

Evander leaned on the side of his car, waiting for her to ask her question.

"If an Idio or Omni die an unnatural death, you say they cease to exist. People are murdered every day, all over the world. How come that hasn't been a big deal to you up until now?"

"Because our deaths are usually natural. Plus, Idios and Omni are protected by a force. They are protected from most things evil and malevolent. The violence you see every day is normal for Common spirits but insignificant in other-worldly aspects. It's the way we are killed that makes the difference. There's no recovery from being burned to a pile of ash and your soul stolen. It's obvious the force doesn't protect us from this murderer."

Evander drove Willow around their small town of Rosaphene without a destination. They were content and comfortable just being in each other's company. Neither of them felt the need to prove anything to each other anymore. Evander was like Zan in that way; he didn't require a lot of attention to be entertained. Willow sat quietly, observing and pondering. She leaned her head on the window, watching her breath fog up the glass, and she kept track of how many times her heart beat. She found Evander's comment about Commons being insignificant a little ignorant. No living being was worth more than the other. Low level or high level, all people, regardless of power or status, were equal in her eyes. She hoped Evander would learn to see that, too.

Evander's cell phone rang. His ringtone was a loud obnoxious beeping that would make plenty of heads turn if they were in public. He pulled over to the side of the road, glanced at the screen, and answered the call without hesitation.

"You'd better be calling with good news, little red," he said.

Willow assumed he was speaking to Rowan. Willow was never happy being in the presence of someone talking on the phone. She hated hearing only one side of the conversation, mostly because she was nosy.

"I'm with Willow, may I bring her?" Evander asked. Not more than a minute later, he sighed and told Rowan that he would see her soon.

"Where are we going?" Willow asked as he tapped the end button on his phone and started his car up again.

"*We* aren't going anywhere. I'm meeting Rowan at my apartment and you're going home."

Willow straightened her back. "Why can't I join you?"

"I mean no disrespect and neither does she, but

she doesn't want you there."

"It's your apartment, you should make that rule. Do you listen to everything she says? Does she own you?"

He slammed on the breaks, causing Willow to lunge forward. She gripped onto the door handle. There were only two other cars on the road and they passed Evander, as he had stopped in the right lane. He glared at her with a look of anger that he had never given her before.

"No." He clenched his jaw. "We aren't meeting up to play board games, or watch movies, or discuss the weather. Rowan believes she is being followed, and my apartment is safe for her. We don't want to put you in danger. Do you understand the severity of this, or do I have to explain further?"

Willow gulped. "Take me home then."

***

When she got home, she went straight to her bedroom to sleep. Her mother woke her up for dinner, which was awkward, as expected. Her father did not have the best day. He stabbed his fork into his food and ate in silence. Her mother hardly looked up from her plate. She might've accidentally eaten a few strands of her own hair.

Willow felt sick to her stomach, not taking more than a few bites before she dumped what she didn't eat into the trash. Typical meal at home, quiet and tense. Maybe they should just start yelling at each other. At least that way it wasn't like they were eating in a morgue.

Her mother didn't protest Willow's ordinary lack of excitement about dinner. She allowed her daughter to slide out of the kitchen and back up into her room.

Willow slept soundly until about three in the morning, when she woke up to a loud bang coming from the kitchen.

She immediately sat up in bed, waiting to hear any more noises, to make sure she wasn't imagining things. Just as her heart rate slowed and she was about to lay back down, she heard glass shatter. She hopped out of bed and grabbed the baseball bat she kept in the back of her closet. Willow tiptoed to her parents' bedroom and pressed an ear against the door. She was surprised to hear faint snoring. The noise in the kitchen hadn't awakened them.

She quietly made her way down the stairs, ready to swing her bat if she were to find a burglar waiting for her. As she got closer to the kitchen, she heard the faucet turn on. She gritted her teeth and braced herself for the worst as she approached the doorway to the kitchen. She entered the dark room and waited for the intruder to give away his position. She heard heavy breathing and an occasional sniffle, so she turned on the light and saw Evander, leaning over the sink with a mug in his hand. A few inches away from him on the floor lay shards of glass and a small puddle of water.

She breathed a sigh of relief and leaned her bat against the wall. "Why did you break into my house?" she whispered angrily. When he turned to her, she noticed his red eyes and swollen face. He parted his lips as if to say something, refusing to give her eye contact, but kept silent. Willow walked up next to him, sidestepping the pieces of glass on the floor.

"What happened?" She placed her hand on his shoulder. She could see that he was tense and having some kind of emotional breakdown.

Evander placed the mug in the sink for someone to wash later. "Rowan is missing."

"What do you mean she's missing?"

"I mean she's gone. She's missing. I met her at my apartment. She was in a panic. After I finally got her to relax, I stepped out for a minute and get some snacks from the store because she asked to stay the night, and I wanted to cheer her up. When I got back, she wasn't there. I looked in every room ten times. When I called her, her phone rang from under my sofa. I drove around for hours, thinking of every place she could possibly have gone, but she's nowhere to be found." Evander took a deep breath. "Then suddenly, I'm standing at your front door and picking your lock like a criminal."

"Why did you pick my lock? Can't you just walk through walls and stuff? You did it at Dr. Everly's office once."

Evander looked her in the eyes. "I'm a Numinist, not a ghost. For some reason, I can't pass through the walls of your house. Something is restricting me. Besides, is now really the time to discuss intangibility?"

"I'm sorry." Willow took her hand away from Evander and very carefully started to pick up the glass from the floor.

Evander bent down to assist her. His eyes were glossy and full of worry, and his voice lost all of its strength. "I tried calling Zan, but he didn't answer. I didn't know where else to go."

Willow threw the glass she'd picked up into the trash. Evander did the same.

"Where's Eira?" she asked.

Evander shook his head. "I have no idea. We don't report to each other. She has her life and I have mine."

"Maybe she could help you find Rowan."

"No," he shouted. "I've never needed her help and I don't ever plan to." He looked lost and exhausted.

"You need some sleep. We'll find Rowan tomorrow."

"I'm not stable enough to be driving."

"You can stay here."

"I don't want to overstay my welcome."

"What are friends for, anyway?"

"You're right. A few hours sleep won't hurt." Evander swallowed. "What if we can't find her?"

"Then we work on Plan B, and if Plan B doesn't work, then we work on Plan C. If Plan C doesn't work, there're still twenty-three more letters in the alphabet."

Evander nodded and gave Willow a hug. She led him up into her room, made sure he was comfortable, grabbed a pillow and blanket from the linen closet and tossed herself on the sofa in the living room. She didn't get much rest, though sometime during the night, she did fall asleep, and she hoped Evander did too.

A few hours later, Willow heard her father

leaving for work. She knew she'd have to get Evander out of her room without drawing attention from her mother. She considered using the small time slot between her father leaving and her mother waking up. But she couldn't bear waking Evander so soon after he'd gone to sleep. Only because her back was hurting and her pain tolerance was low, Willow slowly rose from her makeshift bed and started a fresh pot of coffee. The grumbling noise of the coffee pot kept her awake and alert until she was able to pour herself a cup. The coffee, sadly, made her more nervous than she already was. She knew that if she ate something, her stomach wouldn't hold it down. She sipped on a glass of ice water to calm her jitters.

Her mother walked daintily down the stairs and into the kitchen, not expecting to see Willow sitting cross-legged on the counter top, wide awake.

"What are you doing up so early?" she asked, rubbing her eyes and sauntering over to the coffee pot.

"I could ask you the same thing." Willow struggled to quickly think of a new way to sneak Evander out of the house, with her mother having gotten up earlier than usual.

Her mother sighed but said nothing in response. She sat at the dining table and drank her coffee in discontented silence.

Willow took that opportunity to head upstairs to her room and wake Evander. She cracked her door open just enough to slide in, and then closed it as quietly as possible. Evander's body was twisted, and the comforter was almost off the bed altogether, yet he looked comfortable. Willow could never sleep in that position. She snuck up to him and poked him gently on the shoulder. He didn't wake up. She pushed him a bit, hoping she wouldn't have to resort to aggressive shaking. But he didn't budge. Willow whispered his name and lightly slapped the side of his face. He grunted and groaned, then squinted at her. "What time is it?"

She stared at him creepily. "Time to get up." Anxiously, she grabbed her comforter and started to fold it. "You've gotta get going."

Evander sat up and slumped against the headboard. "A good morning would be nice."

"Good morning. You've gotta go. My mother is awake and we need to start looking for Rowan."

In his eyes, Willow saw a sudden realization come over him. Rowan was still missing, and they had no leads on where she could've gone.

He licked his lips and forced his visibly weak self out of Willow's bed. Evander watched as she paced back and forth, still thinking of a way to sneak him out. She felt scandalous. She had never snuck out of the house before, and had certainly never snuck anyone else *in* or *out*. She wanted to search the Internet for tips on how to get away with it.

"I could always climb out the window," Evander suggested. His morning voice was scratchy and gruff.

She considered his idea. "No. I wouldn't want you to break a leg. We have to get you out the front door...somehow."

Before Evander could say anything in return, Elizabeth yelled Willow's name from downstairs, and she didn't sound happy. Willow shot him a fretful look then ran to see what her mother needed. Willow would be lying if she said she wasn't preparing for her death in those next few minutes.

Out of breath, she approached the living room and played cool. "Is everything okay?"

Elizabeth was peeking out the front window, facing their front yard, coffee in hand, and her face partially covered by the curtains. "There's a car I recognize parked in front of our house. Can you come here and take a look at it?" she asked, scarily calm and her body still.

Willow gulped and followed through with her mother's request, moving aside another curtain and taking a look outside. Evander's car stood out like an alien spaceship. She shook her head. "Strange."

"Very strange." Her mother took a sip from her coffee mug and backed away from the window. "Do you know anything about it, Willow?"

She shook her head again, making herself dizzy. "No, of course not."

"Funny. Because it sure looks like the same car that dropped you off the other day. Are you sure there isn't something you need to tell me?" Elizabeth looked Willow dead in the eyes.

She felt very small and very defeated. "I have no idea why that car is parked outside."

"We'll see about that." Her mother started walking upstairs. She still hadn't put her mug down. Willow trailed after her, already thinking of ways to justify hiding someone in her bedroom. She couldn't come up with anything believable or excusable and started to think of ways to apologize instead.

When Elizabeth reached Willow's bedroom door and turned the knob, Willow thought she was done for. All of her secrets would have to be revealed. She would never be allowed to leave the house again. Grounded for life, kept prisoner in the basement, chained up next to her father's personal flat screen television. She would have to live the rest of her life in regret and embarrassment that she'd let a stranger into the house. She would cry herself to sleep every night and beg for forgiveness from everyone she had ever hurt, lied to, or disappointed.

Willow's life as she knew it, was over.

She should have kicked Evander out as soon as she found him in the kitchen, even though that would've completely contradicted the kind of person she was, always willing to help everyone else before she thought to help herself.

But when the door angled open, what they saw surprised both Willow and her mother. There was no one in the room. Willow's eyes widened and she quickly looked at her mom, who looked skeptical. She made a tour of the room, even looked in the closet, under the bed, and outside her window.

Evander had left without a trace, and Willow couldn't have been more relieved.

"See?" Willow smirked. "I told you I have nothing to do with that stupid car." It scared her how good she was at lying to the woman who had given her life. She hoped, in the end, all of her secrecy would pay off and a murderer would be captured.

Elizabeth sighed and her body relaxed. "I shouldn't have jumped to conclusions." She was still looking around, trying to catch anything out of place in her daughter's bedroom. But the only thing strange was the fact that the bed was made perfectly.

When her mother retreated to sit at the dining room table and read the morning newspaper, Willow quickly washed up. She kissed her mother goodbye and bolted out the front door. The car was gone. Evander had already driven off. Willow had no explanation as to how he was able to escape so quietly. He was a magician. Willow wasn't even sure he was completely human. She considered that maybe he was some kind of alien, after all, and his car really was a spacecraft of some sort. All the training he had put her through was just hallucinations, and he'd been holding her captive ever since she showed up at his apartment the first time. She thought that maybe he spent his time slowly digesting her organs and drinking her blood like people drank protein shakes. It all seemed possible to Willow in that moment, standing on the sidewalk in front of her house, staring blankly ahead. That was until she heard distant honking from a few houses down, coming from Evander, parked, waiting for her to join him on their next life-threatening adventure. She snapped out of her doldrums and dashed down the hill.

"Do I even wanna know how we both got out of this so easily?" Willow asked as she slid in the passenger seat of Evander's car.

He cracked a very small and fragile looking smile. "You sure you don't want me to leave it up to your imagination?"

Willow thought it over. "Tell me some other time. We have to find Rowan."

Chapter 6
THE CENTER OF THE LABYRINTH

Evander drove around for a couple of hours with Willow never leaving his side or sight. Rosaphene wasn't a terribly large town. There weren't many crevices Rowan could've been hiding in. Evander and Willow came to the conclusion that Rowan was not in a public location.

"Is there anything Rowan mentioned that could lead us to where she is?" Willow asked as they exited the art museum for the fifth time that afternoon. Evander sat on one of the steps leading up to the main doors of the museum. The building looked so much different to Willow, knowing she had been inside when no one else was around.

Evander recollected the few hours he spent with Rowan the evening before. "She did mention Ebra."

"What did she say about him?"

"She told me that when she was painting in the warehouse yesterday morning, Ebra appeared over her shoulder. She didn't know where he came from or how he found her, but he started asking her questions."

"What kind of questions?"

"He was trying to weasel himself into my personal life again. Asking about my relationship with Eira, about my relationship with you and Zan." Evander was satisfied with any reason to put blame on Ebra for something that went wrong. He was wary about allowing Willow to help him find Rowan, especially if Ebra was the reason she was missing, but he didn't want to be alone, and he had already included her in his problem when he showed up at her house.

The thought of losing someone else, another someone he was close to, made his chest ache. Loss shadowed him wherever he went, like he could never find peace or hold on to anything good for long. Climbing up a ladder didn't seem worth it to him if he kept getting knocked down. There was no elevator to heaven, but the stairway up was broken, and he was stuck.

***

They drove around town again, no longer

looking for Rowan, but thinking to themselves. Evander didn't tell Willow where they were going, but he was driving to Dr. Everly's office. He wanted to have a serious talk with her about Ebra. After Rowan told Evander about Ebra's invasive questions, she left the warehouse, and she had a terrible feeling in her stomach because she knew she was being followed, but she was too unnerved to turn around to see who was behind her.

Willow, on the other hand, thought about inviting Zan to assist with the search for Rowan. She knew that he was instinctive and would serve as a neutral middle ground because he refused to let himself become emotionally invested in a problem that could be better solved with logic. She didn't know how Evander would feel about that idea.

When Evander parked in the small lot behind Dr. Everly's office, Willow returned her attention to reality and the issue at hand. She didn't ask Evander what they were doing there. He was a fairly reasonable person, and she wouldn't doubt whatever he had planned in order to find their friend. Willow felt like she had been acquainted enough with Rowan to call her a friend.

She followed him around the building and through the front doors. He didn't turn toward her once, not even when they entered Dr. Everly's office. She trailed after him like a lost puppy and watched his body get stiffer by the second. He didn't bother knocking on Eira's office door or even waiting for her to come out; he barged into her office with determination. Evander was practically oozing testosterone.

Dr. Everly was in the middle of a session with a woman who had knotted hair and mascara smeared all over her face. They both turned toward Willow and Evander.

The doctor immediately stood up and straightened her lavender pencil skirt. "Excuse me," she snarled. "You *do not* have permission to be in here. Neither of you."

"She needs to leave." Evander pointed at the crying woman, who clutched her ragged denim purse, one she probably bought from a thrift shop in the 1990s.

Eira looked angered about being spoken to with so little respect. With a wave of a hand, she dismissed her patient, and the woman ran out, terrified. Willow felt as though the woman wouldn't schedule another appointment to see Dr. Everly, not ever again.

Evander kept his distance from Eira at first. "Rowan's missing. Do you have any idea where she is?"

Eira groaned. "Why must you assume I would know where she is? Of course I don't."

Evander rushed toward her and stood mere inches away from her face. "Who do you think you are, Eira? You act like you know it all, been with Ebra for centuries. I don't know if you're oblivious or you're as wicked as he is. I sure hope it's not the latter, or so help me God."

Eira placed a single finger on his chest and pushed him away from her. "Who gave *you*, Evander, the jurisdiction to come into my office and question me? I do not have to answer to you and your little *girlfriend*." Eira eyed Willow.

She saw nothing but rage.

"I need to have a word with Ebra," Evander stated in a voice that could've caused an earthquake. "Where is he?"

Eira folded her hands behind her back. "I thought you wanted nothing to do with him. Besides, I am your superior. I will not give in to your commands."

Evander laughed. "My superior? Oh, tear out my heart now, Eira."

"Don't tempt me," Eira whispered. "Because you know I would. But don't fret, I'll crochet you a new one."

Evander stared at Eira as if thinking of what to say in response, thinking of how to summon a man like Ebra, thinking of what move to make next.

Willow cleared her throat. "Just tell us where we can find Ebra and we'll be out of your hair." She spoke in her strongest tone, but she was nowhere near as intimidating as Evander.

Eira stood slack-jawed, glee glimmering in her eyes. A mocking smile grew slowly on her face. "Where did you find your voice, Willow? Was it buried in your mother's garden under those petunias? Was it in your attic, covered in black widows and glitter? Since when have you been so brave to speak up to me?"

Willow searched the room for her words, hoping they'd be hanging on the walls, but she couldn't find them anywhere. She had never been one to argue as aggressively as her parents or Eira and Evander.

Eira laughed at Willow then turned back to face Evander. "Don't bother looking for the red-headed girl. It wouldn't be worth your time."

Evander's eyes widened, and he grabbed both of Eira's shoulders. She did nothing but smile up at him. He shook her small body and took a deep breath before speaking. "What did you do to her?

Where is she?"

The doctor did nothing. She let herself be shaken and squeezed, knowing he would never truly hurt her. He was frantic, looking for answers not written on her face. It was like her expression had been put on pause, her smile never faded, and her eyes never stopped shining.

Evander noticed she hadn't blinked once since they'd entered her office, and he picked up on what was really going on. He mumbled to himself, let go of her shoulders, and slowly backed away to stand next to Willow, who was trying not to hyperventilate. He wrapped his hand around Willow's upper arm, and gulped. "She's not Eira."

Eira moved quicker than Willow could comprehend. She sprinted at them, still smiling.

In the blink of an eye, Evander flash-transported them somewhere else.

Willow toppled over and fell to the ground. The evil look on Eira's face was fresh on her mind. The room was spinning, and she heard loud ringing for a good two minutes before she heard Evander call her name repeatedly. He was kneeling by her side, holding her by the waist, trying to keep her from passing out. Willow coughed up a bit of blood, and then her vision began to clear. Her body was in an unbelievable amount of pain. She thought she was dying.

Evander turned her onto her side and held her body still. She was trembling and he was trying to keep her as calm as possible in case there was something seriously wrong with her. He remembered, from a previous life, how to help someone if they went into shock. He hoped he wasn't making her worse, and that he wouldn't need to transport them back to the physical world and take her to a hospital. He worried they were in serious danger, and he didn't want to risk losing Willow to Ebra.

As soon as he saw how plastic and dead Eira looked, he knew he had dragged Willow directly into a trap Ebra had set. The woman in the office was an illusion. Ebra knew Evander would go to Eira, looking for Rowan. Ebra knew Evander would have Willow by his side. Ebra was ready to kill them both, mimicking Eira's body to do so more easily.

He flashed himself and Willow to a different realm, one of the safest and most sacred of them all. It was hidden to most. Finding it required extensive will and knowledge of the many spiritual realms accessible. It was, as far as Evander knew, protected by a force called the *Praesidio et Potentiam Deitatis;* the same force that was supposed to protect all Idios and Omni. The realm they were in was called *Centrum Labyrinth*, better known as *The Center of the Labyrinth*.

Willow slowly began to breathe normally again, and her body stabilized. She turned her head slightly to look up at Evander's face. He had his eyes closed, as if he was in a trance. Willow let out a soft groan, and his eyes immediately flickered open. They were as bright and blue as ever.

"You were hurt. I was scared." He sounded robotic, but he was just coming down from a rush of adrenaline.

Willow blinked at him, sat up slowly, and looked around the room they were in, still thinking about the last thing she saw: Eira.

Evander smiled. His hair was all over the place, and his eyes were as glossy as they had been the night before. He looked up, around and back at Willow, who was registering reality again.

"Where are we?"

Evander let out a nervous laugh. "We're in the heart of *everything*. We're in the heart of *creation*, of *life*, of mortality and divinity. This is the center of it all." He rose from the floor and spun slowly and dramatically in a circle, gesturing around them.

Willow looked up and saw a never-ending

wooden spiral staircase that composed the walls around them. The room was large and circular, books on endless shelves, and doors of all shapes, sizes, and colors on every floor the staircase led to. She was on the first floor where there was a single door covered in plush maroon velvet. It had a fancy golden lock and knob. Thick black books with golden numbers printed on the spines surrounded the Velvet Door.

"Is this some kind of library?" Willow asked, still sitting on the floor, afraid to stand up and get dizzy again.

Evander walked over to the first shelf on the right of the Velvet Door and slid out the book numbered *one*. He handed it to Willow and she opened it to the first page. She wasn't shocked to see names and dates, handwritten on pristine white pages in minuscule fonts.

Evander smiled down at Willow, who traced her fingers along the page. "In these books are the names of every Common Spirit who lived and chose to die, as opposed to those who chose to be reincarnated to evolve."

"How many names are here?"

"A lot. I can't know for sure, it's hard to keep track. The archive of the Commons who chose to be reincarnated is on the next floor. Those would be the names of the people who are currently living to evolve into Idios."

"Where are the names of the current Idios and Omni that are alive?"

Evander walked toward a podium on the other side of the room, directly across from the Velvet Door. Willow got to her feet and followed him.

On the podium sat three golden books; one was much thicker than the others, the one on the left; Evander pointed to that one first. "This one lists the names of Idios that are alive. There aren't many."

Then he pointed to the book in the middle. "This one lists the names of Looscents that are alive. There are even less."

Finally, he pointed to the book on the right. "That one lists the names of Numinists that are alive. When an Idio or Omni get reincarnated, their names get re-written to the name they were given at their most recent birth. The same goes for the Commons that are currently evolving. But now, the names of those who have been murdered just disappear completely. The next time new names will be written in is when a Common evolves into an Idio, and the next time a Looscent is born or evolves into a Numinist." Evander paused to crack his knuckles. "There is an uneven number of Looscents and Numinists now. It's no longer a fair cycle, and it probably never will be again. These murders threw everything out of whack."

"Is my name in there?"

"Somewhere, yes."

If Willow had been alive as long as Evander, and she was in the same spot he was in, she would've been more worried about protecting herself than going after the person or presence that was killing her friends and others. She felt that would've been a very selfish decision, but she didn't think she would put her own life *that* much at risk.

She had a newfound respect for Evander. She hadn't known him long, but she looked up to him and trusted him as much as she trusted Zan, possibly even more in some ways. Maybe that was naïve of her, maybe it was natural instinct, or maybe it was a combination of both.

The heart of creation. She stared up at the infinite number of stairs, wondering if they led to an even more spectacular place like the throne of God. *If only everyone knew something like this exists.* She took notice of the Velvet Door and walked to it. She smoothed the soft fabric with her hand; she had always loved the way velvet felt. Evander came up behind her and tossed his heavy arm around her shoulders.

"I have no idea where this door leads to. No one does. Many have tried unlocking it and breaking it down, but it never opens."

Willow embraced the mystery of the Velvet Door. Everything about it excited her. Clarence would be proud.

They spent some time looking through the books on the first floor and read names out loud. She never once questioned why they were in that room in the first place. She claimed that she hated how often people asked *why*, when she had been one of those people too, always wanting to know the answers to everything. She decided to take the advice Evander had given her once, and just let things be as they were, without question.

Evander lost track of the time. Even though a long time in a different realm may have been just a few minutes, or even seconds, in the physical world, he didn't want them to be gone too long. He just needed to escape Ebra and get his thoughts in order. And now he grew worried about Zan, too.

"We have to get back. Rowan is still missing. There is work to be finished." He put the book he held back in its place then approached Willow.

She took hold of his hand. "I'm ready when you are." She gave his hand a soft, reassuring squeeze, and soon they were nothing but atoms and energy, traveling through the air and across spiritual planes, one in the same with the universe.

***

Evander transported himself and Willow back to his apartment. It was just as colorful as Willow remembered it, though the paintings on his wall had changed. She had first seen them both as blank canvases, but with her new and improved perspective, she saw one was an elaborate portrait of a red fox, and the other was an acrylic painting of dead red roses. Rowan had signed them in the bottom right corners. She watched Evander search through his kitchen drawers and underneath his couch cushions.

"What are you looking for?"

He was crouched down on the floor now, patting the carpet with his hands. "My apartment is a mess," he grumbled.

Willow didn't notice any messes. No dirty dishes sat in his sink, no pairs of shoes were visible, and the entire living room smelled like lemon scented cleaning products. It smelled so clean, it was almost disgusting.

Evander stood up and ran into the other room. Willow heard closet doors slam shut and a few bangs against the walls. When he came out, he carried a very ugly vintage lamp with a baby blue lampshade covered in faded yellow sticky notes with words written on them in Latin.

"Nothing is right. All of my protection sachets and crystals are gone." Evander held the lamp at his side and slumped his shoulders, looking heartbroken.

She looked around, noticing the lack of crystals she'd seen earlier. She carefully stepped closer to Evander and took the lamp and placed it gently on the kitchen bar, even though she wanted to throw it in a dumpster.

Evander sat on his couch, held his head in his hands, and sobbed.

She wished she knew how to console people when they were crying. She could handle everything except human tears and very ill children. Sitting next to him, she patted his back. When he didn't stop sobbing for five minutes, she slid her phone out of her pocket and texted Zan. *Drop everything you're doing and get to Evander's apartment.* She wasn't sure what Zan could do or say to help the situation, but she figured it would be better for him to not be out in public and vulnerable to any attacks.

None of us should be alone for too long.

Evander stopped crying and stared solemnly at the paintings on his wall. Even when someone knocked at his front door, he didn't flinch. He looked at Willow questioningly. She gave him a friendly smile and answered his door to reveal Zan, out of breath, in uniform for work, and with purple contacts in place.

"You never told me what his apartment number was. An old French woman almost beat me with a spoon." He noticed Willow wasn't in the mood to laugh.

She signaled for him to step inside, and she shut the door behind him. Right away, his eyes drifted to Evander, who looked defeated and just straight-up depressed. He had a good reason to be.

Willow filled Zan in. "Rowan is missing. And Evander has been muttering about some sachets and crystals that have gone missing."

Zan tossed his jacket on the floor, stood directly in front of Evander, and lifted his despondent friend's head with a finger under his chin. "Oh no," Zan said. "You've got a bad case of the Glum Bug. We need to get you some chicken nuggets and a strawberry milkshake, stat."

Evander squinted at Zan and swiped his hand away. He scowled at Zan and Willow then weakly rose from the couch. "Do both of you think this is a time for jokes? My best friend is *missing*, Ebra mimicked Eira and almost got Willow and myself killed, and my apartment isn't protected anymore. It probably hasn't been for a while now, but it took me this long to notice, and I have *failed... Again.*"

Zan shook his head at Evander. "I don't know what's going on, and I can't take the feeling of failure away, but throwing your anger on your friends isn't going to solve anything. Now what's this about Rowan?"

Evander lowered his voice. "She's been gone since last night. Ebra might've been following her, so I brought her here then left her alone. If I had noticed my crystals and sachets were missing, I wouldn't have done that, and she probably wouldn't have disappeared. Now we're all sitting ducks." His swollen eyes searched for something to lock on, but they kept wandering.

There was a moment of silence. All three of them dipped their heads and took a few deep breaths. Evander sat back down and Willow dropped to the floor and crossed her legs like a preschooler. If Evander was right, they were royally screwed.

After some time, they were all sitting cross-legged on the floor in a circle. Evander mentioned something to Willow about convincing Eira, if he could get a hold of her, to cancel all sessions with her until it was safe enough to go back. In addition, Evander couldn't trust Eira again, and didn't want to endanger Willow. There were no more reasons for him and Willow to visit her office and discuss any problems at hand.

Zan laid a hand on Evander's shoulder. "I'll take a few days off work to help find Rowan."

Evander set his hand on top of Zan's. "Thank you. I don't want to be alone on this one."

"Would you like me to stay with you for the time being?"

Evander nodded. "Please. And Willow, do me a favor. Lay low. Don't draw attention to yourself. Stay home until it's absolutely necessary to leave."

Because she hated being at home, she was hesitant to agree. "I guess I can do that. We all need to stay as safe as possible. Don't do anything you wouldn't let *me* do."

If they wanted to save themselves and each other, they knew they had to be smart. Or at least smarter than Ebra. All of their fingers were pointing at him as the murderer.

***

Willow kept her promise and didn't leave the house for three days. She locked herself in her room and only came out for meals and to convince her parents she wasn't doing drugs or building a bomb. Evander mimicked Eira, called Elizabeth, and canceled all their appointments due to *a sudden vacation to the Caribbean.*

Elizabeth wasn't as skeptical as Willow had expected.

Zan and Evander kept in close contact with her. They scoured a few realms, The Veil, and even went as far as driving to several towns near Rosaphene, but Rowan was nowhere to be found.

Willow used some of her free time to practice shifting, which she was close to mastering. She found that being a cat was much easier than being human. Sitting on her window seat as a cat was much more relaxing. The sun directly hit her as she rested her head on the flower-patterned cushion. Willow also took some time to catch up on organizing her room. But mostly, she rested up a lot, as if preparing herself for some kind of battle to come.

She had never been so disconnected from the world. It was scary, not stepping out to get fresh air or communicating with fellow humans and making small talk about the weather or the news. She never expected to long for interaction with strangers. Her mother and father, for the most part, left her alone. They had their own troubles to deal with. She had a bad feeling that they were giving up on her but didn't have much time to focus on that because she had bigger things to worry about. Being the world's greatest daughter, at that point, wasn't at the top of her priorities list.

It felt strange that she hadn't seen Clarence. They usually saw each other once a week, usually at Crossroads, but also at the library and park. Part of why she hadn't seen him could've been because she just hadn't been out and about enough to run into him. With all that was going on, she couldn't visit The Art District for a bagel or coffee and walk around. She had to lay low all day.

She knew she wasn't alone, but she felt like that at times. Evander was her friend, and so was Zan, but everyone was immersed in their own business and issues; Willow was somehow just in the middle of it all. She wasn't complaining, but she missed conversations that didn't revolve around existential crises. She missed conversations about books and what color the sky was, or about scavenger hunts and kale shake recipes that Clarence would talk about excitedly. Her life felt thrilling and scarily empty at the same time.

***

Early Monday morning, Willow was eating breakfast, which consisted of scrambled eggs and burnt turkey bacon, on her window seat, watching the birds fly around and the leaves on the big mulberry tree fall to the ground.

Meanwhile, Evander was in a screaming match with Zan back at the apartment.

"I don't know how you expect to cover millions of realms in the course of a few hours," Zan yelled, waving his hands around like a madman. He was sleep deprived and growing frustrated with Evander's impossible ideas to find Rowan. He forgot what it was like, living with a man who dreamed impractical dreams.

Evander's palms were pressed together as if he was about to pray. "I don't expect to cover *millions* of realms, Zan. I'm just saying, maybe we need to look in some *more* places."

Zan rolled his eyes and slammed his fist on the kitchen bar, startling Evander. "What is *wrong* with you? We will *not* find her today, and probably not tomorrow. We need a better plan."

Evander took a deep breath and refused to continue arguing. "Why are you so filled with hate? You used to glow golden. Are you aware of how much you've dimmed? Your light is dull, flickering." He made grabby motions with his hands in front of Zan's face.

Zan wasn't amused. He grabbed both of Evander's wrists and held them still. "It starts and ends with you, my friend. I'm not driving myself to death for *you*."

"Really?" Evander raised his eyebrows. "If not, then for whom? Willow? Both of us know how much you care about her. I care about her too, but why would either of us have to prove ourselves to her? She trusts us already. You could buy a plane ticket and flee the country with her. That might keep you two safe for a little while. But you've chosen to stick around with *me*, to work with *me*, why, if you weren't trying to prove yourself to me. You say you could care less about my opinion of you, but yet you're still here."

Zan let go of Evander's wrists.

Evander palmed Zan's cheek. "You could keep trying to build those walls up higher, but they'll have to come down eventually." Evander backed away and exited his own apartment, leaving Zan to make another decision. Stay and let his walls collapse, or leave with his pride and bitterness toward the past, possibly forever.

Evander didn't walk down the hallway of his apartment complex and down the stairs with a smile. He wasn't proud of the ultimatum he was forced to make regarding Zan. He just hoped everything would work out in the end. That was how life often worked. People lived on hope for the good and for the better, winging their way through fights with loved ones, fights they would rather not have. If only they could wake up and everything went the way they wanted it. But where was the fun in a guarantee of peace until the end of time?

He hopped in his car and made his way toward Willow's house. If Zan wanted to find him, he would know where to look.

Willow had finished her breakfast when she saw Evander's flashy car pull up into her driveway. She quickly put her plate on the window seat and raced down the stairs. Her mother was lounging on the sofa, reading a book. Without saying a word to her mother, she ran out into her front yard and approached Evander as he climbed out of his car.

"You can't be here right now. You didn't warn me you were coming."

Evander said nothing and walked up the pathway toward the front door where Elizabeth stood without a clue as to what was happening.

Willow chased after him. Her face suddenly felt very hot.

He stuck his hand out for Elizabeth to shake. "We've met. I'm Evander. I'm coming inside."

She was at a loss for words, stepped to the side, and let him and her daughter in the house. She eyed Willow as she followed Evander in. Willow pretended not to notice.

"So here's the deal." Evander leaned on the staircase railing. "Zan's got some choices to make and Rowan is still missing in action. Eira is I-don't-know-where, and Ebra is still out there somewhere, and man, I could really go for some hot tea right now."

Willow folded her arms. "What plan letter are we on?" she asked, still ignoring her mother's persistent glare.

"Plan Veh. We're so past the English alphabet, we're on the Enochian one now." Evander clapped his hands together. "Now how about that tea?"

She pointed to the kitchen. Evander winked at her and went on to make himself some tea. She heard a few cupboards open and close, then the pantry, the sink faucet, and buttons chirp on the microwave.

Elizabeth stepped around Willow and stared at her face, which was as blank as a sheet. Random appearances from Evander were normal to her, but not to her mother.

"What in the world is going on here?" she hissed through her shiny white teeth.

Willow bit her lip, then, "Evander can be a bit dramatic. Everything's fine. Promise." She smiled awkwardly at her mother, and speed-walked into the kitchen.

Evander stood in the middle of the room, sipping his tea, both hands firmly gripping the thick clay mug Willow had made in a summer pottery class. His shoulders were tensed and his hands trembled. She mouthed *are you okay*, and Evander shook his head. Her mother appeared in the doorway and hovered there as if waiting for her unspoken questions to be answered.

Evander cleared his throat and steadied his hands. "I apologize, Mrs. Ferring, for bursting in. I'm going through some critical situations lately, and your daughter has been a tremendous help."

Elizabeth nodded slowly and glared at Evander as if studying him. "I see."

Willow ground her teeth together and kept her eyes set on Evander, knowing he would console her mother.

He shot her a million-dollar smile. "Willow is in good hands. Zan and I would never get her into any kind of trouble."

Her mother nodded again but quicker. "That isn't much consolation."

The three of them stood in an awkward silence until they heard the sound of the front door open and slam shut. Willow's mother spun around and gasped. Zan walked past her. Evander put his half-empty mug of tea into the sink as Zan rushed toward him. Just as he was about to say something that would earn him a slap across the face, Zan hugged him.

"I'm staying. You're right. I hate to admit it," he said breathlessly, like he had run all the way there from the apartment.

Evander gulped and nodded vigorously. "All right. You're gonna have to serenade me with a song and dance first, though."

Zan laughed at Evander's remark and let his head fall onto Evander's shoulder. Evander patted his back and smiled. When the air in the room thinned out, she walked over to them, and they all hugged long enough to make up for a thousand hugs that had never happened. They would treasure these few moments together for a very long time. These were moments of unification, complete trust, and most importantly, love. Not knowing what was about to come next, they would need these moments to hold on to.

When they pulled away from each other and faced their turbulent reality once again, Willow's mother was still in the room. She eavesdropped on their conversations like the protective parent she was. Willow needed to get ready and carry on with her journey. Without stating what she was doing, she left the kitchen and went upstairs to change out of her pajamas, leaving Evander and Zan to figure out how to prove to her mother that they weren't going to get Willow killed or handcuffed... Ergo, they had to lie. They had done plenty of lying before, so it wasn't a challenge anymore. But they'd be kidding themselves if they said they weren't just a *little* scared of Willow's mother.

Evander gave her a spiel about how he was having *relationship* problems and needed *good friends to surround him.* When she asked how he and Zan knew each other, Zan said they were friends throughout elementary and middle school, but lost touch and had recently reconnected. They knew better than to overcompensate, and they were pretty convincing. Elizabeth didn't say much, but she did listen, and argued none.

When Willow returned downstairs, everyone was gathered in the living room by the front door. As she joined them, her mother sighed. "Don't do anything stupid. Be careful." She gave Willow a hug.

Willow told her mother that she'd stay out of trouble, then followed Evander and Zan out to the car.

Chapter 7
ASHES, ASHES

Willow relaxed in the back seat of Evander's car while he and Zan discussed more ways to go about finding Rowan. Evander decided to visit Eira's office one more time in hopes that what had happened the last time he was there with Willow wouldn't happen again. They needed to contact Eira in order to address Ebra. He was masterful at hiding and he hardly ever let his guard down. It would be too difficult to find him without the help of someone who knew him well.

It was one of the last warm days of the year, perfect for a sugar-loaded latte to make Willow feel good about herself. As the car sped through the empty streets of Rosaphene, she leaned her head against the window and daydreamed about the winter to come. She was looking forward to the snow and wearing thick colorful scarves. She was excited to go ice-skating with her friends and eat fattening food on Thanksgiving. The winter always made her feel domesticated, and maybe that wasn't such a bad thing.

On every New Year's Eve, her father would tell her to look to the stars instead of the future, because the stars would never leave her like days gone by. She would tell him that she needed the future to look to, or else she would have nothing to aim for. He would shake his head and tell her to just aim for the stars. The stars. Always the stars. She thought he knew something she didn't. Seemed like everyone knew something she didn't, and maybe that wasn't such a bad thing either.

Evander made a sharp turn into the parking lot of Dr. Everly's office, jolting Willow out of her thoughts.

"Are we gonna walk in with guns blazing, or what?" Zan asked.

Evander mumbled something inaudible in response and they all hopped out of the car.

The energy surrounding Dr. Everly's office was dark and heavy. The exterior walls felt uninviting. She could tell that Evander had a difficult time getting himself to open the front door. His and Zan's faces lost color except for the dark veins under their eyes. Willow imagined her own face didn't look much different.

As they entered Eira's office, it was as if they were transported to a hell-like twilight zone. The waiting room was unlit and dead silent. When a young blonde woman about Willow's height walked out of Eira's office, they were all startled. Thick framed glassed rested on her piglet-like nose, and in her hand was a clipboard holding a few loose sheets of paper.

"Who are you?" Evander demanded, though not brave enough to step toward her.

"Lorelei."

Lorelei had a German accent and a tone of voice that could make the strongest individual worship and serve her.

Evander shook his head. "My name's Evander. What are you doing here?"

"I am Dr. Everly's new assistant. What are *you* doing here?"

"Paying my friend a casual visit. Where is she?"

Lorelei checked her clipboard. "Busy."

"Busy doing what?"

"Work."

"Working where?"

"Elsewhere."

Evander pushed his hair back, only to have it fall back onto his forehead. He looked stressed and ready to strangle someone. "We need to see her."

Lorelei giggled. "You cannot see Eira. She is taking care of...*business*."

Zan noticed the necklace she was wearing. It was a bright pink choker that had a striking similarity to a dog's collar. A silver circular charm hung loosely on the front, accentuating her defined collarbones. He elbowed Evander and nodded toward her, implying that Evander needed to look at her more closely. He saw her choker, too, and soon he was on the same page as Zan.

Zan smiled. "How did you keep yourself hidden?"

"What do you mean by that?" Lorelei made an innocent expression.

"Is it the collar? All Idios and Omni are completely aware of each other, especially when someone is in their animal form. I've never heard any bells ring. I didn't even hear one today. How do you do it?"

She held her clipboard against her midsection, squeezing it so hard that her knuckles turned white. "I don't know what you're talking about."

"I still have a scar from when you bit my ankle. Thanks for that."

Lorelei huffed and smacked her plump pink lip-gloss drenched lips. "None of you are permitted to be here. You have to go now."

Evander slipped a finger into her collar and yanked her toward him. His occasional outbursts of aggression often worried Willow, but at the moment it seemed appropriate so she didn't address him about it.

Lorelei squealed and tried to tear herself away, teeth clenched and sparkly. When he unclasped her collar, she tumbled to the floor, gasped for air, and coughed from the strain Evander had put on her neck.

They all heard the jingle of a bell. Lorelei's collar must've had a spell cast on it. An object that could keep a person's identity and true form hidden from the rest of the world had never been heard of until Lorelei's collar was discovered. They never did figure out how she or Ebra did it, or obtained the kind of power to do it in the first place. Evander decided to keep it. He would toss it in the drawer in the nightstand by his bed.

For now, Evander held the collar with his thumb and pointer finger and dangled it out in front of him as if it were contaminated. He folded it up and slipped it into his pocket before Lorelei was able to snatch it from him.

Lorelei, cheeks red and swollen, tossed her clipboard to the floor and ambled seductively toward Willow. Willow tilted her body backwards when the tip of Lorelei's nose bumped hers. In her peripheral vision, Willow saw Evander and Zan physically preparing to pounce on Lorelei if she dared to do anything violent.

Lorelei moved a few strands of hair behind Willow's ear and leaned forward. "You three are making a big mistake," she whispered.

Evander moved close to Lorelei, but before he could grab her and pull her backward, Lorelei spun around and wrapped her skinny fingers around his wrist. Zan moved in to attack, but she immediately grasped Willow by her neck, and all three of them disappeared.

Zan started heaving, close to tearing his hair out, alone in Eira's waiting room with only Lorelei's clipboard left behind. He moaned in anger and punched the air before running back outside, but not before thinking twice about whether or not to pick up the clipboard and see what she had written down. He ultimately decided not to. He wasn't in the best state of mind. His friends had just been kidnapped.

Zan ran to Evander's car, remembered he didn't have keys for it, and screamed. A few birds flew out of trees, startled by his outburst of anger. With his entire body shaking, he started to walk away from Eira's office building.

***

Evander and Willow woke up sometime after they were abducted, each tied and handcuffed to a chair, seated at a long table in a moody dining room. The walls were covered in plum wallpaper pattered with diamonds of various sizes. Pictures of people from Victorian times hung hauntingly. It was impossible to feel like they weren't being stared at constantly. Four long black candles were placed in a row on the table, with a short crystal vase directly in the center, holding black feathers that were covered in dust. The chandelier above them swung slightly, causing the small crystals to clink and make low chiming noises. Willow tried pulling free from the cuffs binding her hands and the ropes holding her forearms to the armrests.

"This place feels familiar," Evander said, looking around the room, examining the eerie décor.

Willow agreed that the place did feel familiar. High pitched screaming and whining from behind the only door was very unsettling. The door opened—a small bell jingled—and in strode a slender, petite short-haired girl with boyish facial features. Two large men in suits, who looked like clones of Ebra, held her by both arms. They pulled out another chair and roughly pushed the girl onto it, cuffing her the same way Evander and Willow were restrained. The men left as quickly as they came. They shut and locked the door behind them. The girl slumped over, her head down and breathing heavily. She looked malnourished.

"What's your name?" Evander asked the girl.

She weakly lifted her head. "Mirele." She had an English accent and a voice full of sorrow.

Evander blinked once. "How long have you been here, Mirele?"

"Weeks. Three at least."

Evander groaned. "How are they treating you?"

Mirele shrugged. "They bring me in here once a day, tie me to a chair and expect me to eat. Even if I could reach my fork, I wouldn't dare touch their food. I've accepted that I will die here. There's another girl here. I've only seen her once, about a day or two ago. She spit in a guard's face, and I haven't seen her since. Her name was Rowan, I believe."

Evander gulped and let go of a breath he didn't know he was holding. He leaned back and turned to Willow. "This is weird," he whispered. "The taunting with the food, I don't get it. Why wait until they eat? Why not just *kill* them as soon as they get here and get it over with?"

"Maybe they want their hostages to give up," Willow said, "They tease them, keep them locked up until they break. Sedating them is too easy, just killing them is too easy. They want to feel powerful and cause the captive to choose death over life."

Evander dug his short nails into the armrests. "Where do they keep you?" he asked Mirele.

"A small bedroom. There aren't any windows or a doorknob on the inside." She smiled faintly. "I take it you have a good idea of what's going on."

Evander smirked. "Sadly, yes." He felt sorry for Mirele. He read her to be a Looscent, like Willow. She must not have met her guide yet. "The energy here feels similar to the energy of your home," Evander whispered to Willow. A force restricted him from transporting out or using any other power.

His comment made Willow feel uneasy, because she felt the same way, only she didn't want to believe it. She thought about her parents and hoped they were doing okay. Had her mother told her father about what happened between her,

Zan, and Evander in the kitchen? She desperately wanted them to believe that she was safe, even if she wasn't.

The guards soon came back into the dining room, carrying three plates of food on fine china. They placed each plate in front of their three hostages and stood watching them. Neither of the two Ebra-Clones said a word, but Willow noticed that Evander was eyeing one in particular, with a look of sheer anger.

Evander nodded toward the guard he had been in a staring contest with. "I need a little help cutting my steak, buddy." The guard strode over without hesitation. He picked up the fork and steak knife by Evander's plate and very slowly, cut the steak into bite-size pieces. A la Rowan, Evander looked up, spat in the guard's face, and then proceeded to bite his arm. Willow screamed as both guards un-cuffed and forcibly dragged Evander out of his chair without any further fight from him. As they tied his hands around his back, he shot Willow one last smile and winked. The guards muscled him out of the room. She feared that would be the last time she would ever see him.

Mirele looked fearful for him, too, even shed a tear on the assumption that the guards would kill him and burn his remains.

Instead, they dragged him through the mansion-like prison and directly to the basement where they pushed him down a flight of stairs and locked the door. He picked himself up off the dirty concrete floor and looked around the dark, humid, and giant basement. He navigated around shelves and boxes, old furniture and stacks of books, until he reached a brick wall. A small window was placed high up, not big enough to climb out of, but big enough for light to seep through.

"Evander, this was not one of your best ideas," he said to himself, sighing at his stupidity. He couldn't fathom why he would've even come to the conclusion that *doing exactly what Rowan did and leaving Willow all alone in danger*, would be a fantastic plan. He turned his head to the right and saw a floor-to-ceiling chain link cage settled in a corner, and then he noticed something moving and rushed toward it. He may have tripped over a rat or a similarly sized creature along the way. As he got closer, the person in the cage turned to him and recognized who he was right away.

"Evander? Is that you?" she yelled.

He couldn't help but smile. "You're not dead."

Rowan let herself out of the cage and ran to him with open arms. She hugged him, and he only wished he could hug her back.

"Why didn't they tie you up?" he asked her when she pulled away. Her wildly red hair was all over the place.

"It isn't that hard to break free. There're enough sharp objects down here to grind a rope against." Rowan helped Evander get untied, and they made their way back to the stairs Evander was thrown down.

Rowan remarked, "These guards. They're not the smartest, are they? They didn't even come to check on me, not even once."

Evander laughed. "You know one of them is Eira, right? She's just mimicking Ebra."

Rowan's eyes widened, and for a moment, she looked greatly amused. "Well, I coulda' seen that coming from a million miles away. Ebra is obviously the big man in charge, but *Eira*, being on his side and all, not hard to figure."

He shrugged. "Deep inside I already knew she was behind this with Ebra. We still don't know half of what's going on, though. All we know is that this is where they keep us until they kill us. How, why, and when they kill us is a different story. What we do about it is another one."

Evander inspected the lock on the door to the basement and wiggled the handle a few times, making sure it was really locked. The entire door looked flimsy enough to kick down, but he wasn't in the mood to draw attention to any escape attempt.

"I guess you've already tried picking the damn thing," he said, wiggling the handle again.

Rowan raised an eyebrow. "Pick the lock? I can't pick a lock."

Evander turned to her. He could've sworn he had taught her how. He was astounded that she hadn't tried to pick her way out of the basement.

They scoured the basement for thin, pointy items. Rowan found a bobby pin bookmarking a page in an old encyclopedia.

He asked her to stay quiet as he worked the lock pins. He couldn't believe that Ebra and Eira were mindless enough to not consider that someone would eventually escape from their basement. *Unless not many people ended up here, and they really aren't tactical, after all. Or they placed people in easily escapable places on purpose to test them.* Either way, Evander was determined to get out of there with both Rowan and Willow in tow.

After a short while, he finally heard the lock give, and he was able to turn the doorknob with no force at all. *This was too easy*. The mansion was quiet. Neither Ebra nor Eira were anywhere in sight. Evander had kept track of where the dining room was and went there first, hoping Willow and Mirele were still there. Rowan followed him around without question.

The mansion was the epitome of gothic. The flooring alternated from checkered tiling to dark hardwood. The air conditioner must've been turned up to full blast; it was absolutely freezing. Evander had to concentrate to keep his teeth from chattering and he constantly rubbed his hands together.

Rowan didn't speak to him at all. She had no questions or explanations for him, or even exclamations of gratefulness that he'd found her. Her attitude or lack thereof was out of the ordinary. Evander disregarded his concerns for the sake of keeping his goal on course to find Willow.

Before Evander opened the double doors to the dining room, he held onto the doorknob for a few seconds and shut his eyes. He was trying to manifest just enough energy to mimic Ebra, just like Eira did. But he still wasn't able to access any power. He and Rowan might as well have been Commons roaming that mansion.

It was then that something finally occurred to him. He had never escaped, not really. It was all set up from the beginning: Rowan going missing and finding a bobby pin in that overcrowded and disorganized basement, and Rowan not showing any signs of anxiousness or stress, which he knew she was very prone to do. She had been part of Ebra and Eira's plan for a while, if not the entire time. He felt naïve, and sick to his stomach. He had known Rowan for centuries and to think that she succumbed to some kind of evil was disappointing and frightening. He wished that one of the powers that came with being a Numinist was the ability to see people for who they really were.

Evander opened his eyes, and tried not to show Rowan any shift in character. He relaxed and opened the door, expecting to see Willow still sitting at the table, but the room was empty. Willow and Mirele had already been moved. He whispered a string of profanities under his breath and collected his thoughts.

He turned to Rowan. "I need to find the bedrooms they keep their hostages in."

"They're upstairs. You lookin' for something?"

Evander made trigger-pulling motion with his thumb and pointer finger, and traipsed up the tall, shiny staircase. As he got closer to the second floor, he heard hushed chatter coming from a room to his right. The door was wide open. He was careful sneaking up to it, unlike Rowan, who walked around the mansion like it was her own. She was making it too obvious that she wanted to get caught, or wanted *Evander* to get caught.

He peeked carefully into the master bedroom, where he was able to see half of Ebra, the *real* Ebra, sitting on the bed with *Butch* the dog, sound asleep next to him. Ebra had his back facing the door, staring out an oversized water-droplet-stained window. Eira was on the other side of the room, staring at herself in the mirror of her vanity like the narcissist she was.

Ebra dipped his head and rolled one of the sleeves of his white shirt up to his elbow. From Evander's perspective, he couldn't see much. But Ebra had a syringe, and he injected a purple glowing substance straight into his veins. His body reacted less and less every time he did it. It was painful at first, shooting an actual soul into his body, feeling the energy colliding with his own. It was his drug of choice.

Eira stood.

Evander pulled back. He pressed his body against the hallway wall and moved away from the bedroom door, leery and watchful of his surroundings. Watchful of Rowan and her intentions. They stared at each other, both unwilling to crack under each other's pressure. Rowan was on to him, as he was on to her.

He contemplated on which of the many doors to open. It felt like Russian roulette. He could open the wrong door and the fury of a thousand hornets could be unleashed. Of course he'd knock first, but that wouldn't guarantee that the hornets would be any less angry.

Experimenting, he closed his eyes again and began walking forward, running his hands over the wall and doors. He was waiting until he felt energy resonate inside him to knock on a door instead of picking one at random. He would be able to feel Willow's presence somewhere since they were connected metaphysically, just as he was able to feel Zan even when they were apart. At first, every room felt empty, the walls cold, and the energy nefarious. He was about to second guess himself about being able to feel anything at all, considering the circumstances, but a tingle in his chest gave him hope and he kept moving forward.

The tingle became stronger as he moved closer to a door at the end of the hall. Along with that tingle, he also felt sorrow and uneasiness. He knew it was Willow. She was very spiritually expressive of her feelings. So much so that even someone who wasn't connected to her would be able to feel her presence. She was far from being afraid to let the universe know how she felt, and it was striking. Evander opened his eyes and looked all around him. Rowan was gone. Vexed with her, he cracked his knuckles and sent some very heated vibes her way.

He knocked quietly on the door that he felt Willow was behind, but she didn't respond. He knocked a few more times, and still no response. He tried using the same bobby pin he used before to pick the lock on the door, but failed after a few long minutes. The lock was difficult to work with, and he didn't want to waste any more time. Before he could think of another plan, Rowan appeared behind him and placed a hand on his shoulder. Evander spun around to face her and yelped. He immediately slapped his hand over his mouth.

Rowan's doe eyes were glistening with surprise. Ebra stepped out of the master bedroom and checked down the hall, suspicious at Evander's quickness to give himself away. Evander immediately made eye contact with him. Ebra grinned as he strode to Evander, both hands in his pockets and standing monstrously tall. Evander gulped, Rowan breathed a heavy sigh, and Ebra whistled until he stood just mere inches away from Evander.

Misguidance gets the best of everyone. Humankind is very easy to manipulate; Evander knew that well enough. *Which is why he decided not to hold Rowan's misguided decision to betray him against her.* She and Evander were close in spiritual age, but Rowan's world experience was far below Evander's. Her naivety wasn't something to be punished. Rowan's attempt to see the greater good in any situation was worthy of praise.

Rowan's eyes darted from Evander to Ebra nervously. Some kind of switch flipped inside her to empathize with her lifelong friend instead of the man who wanted nothing other than to see the world burn. She turned her back to Evander and placed both palms on Ebra's chest. She tilted her head back far enough to look him in the eyes, and she pleaded for him to spare Evander's life.

"I can't let you kill him," she whispered.

Ebra couldn't have been less shocked. He slowly pulled a gold lighter out of his pocket. Rowan fluttered her eyelids shut and removed her hands from Ebra's body. She kept them at her sides. Evander took a few steps back. Fear had found a home inside of him.

Ebra flicked the lighter, and with a powerful

force, he tossed it straight toward Rowan's torso. Her body became engulfed in flames.

Evander widened his eyes at the sight of Rowan burning away to nothing right in front of his face. He cried for her and hoped she wasn't in pain. Evander couldn't see Ebra behind the flames that ravaged his friend's body. The flames changed from orange, to red, and to a dark maroon color. From dark maroon they changed to violet, and from violet to a vivid and blinding purple. Rowan's body quickly became a small pile of ash below a lingering pillar of purple light.

He reached out to touch the glowing light that refused to fade out. When it came in contact with his skin, his ears filled with a loud ringing unlike anything he had ever heard before.

Ebra stepped toward the light with an empty syringe and sucked the light of Rowan's soul into it.

As Evander became accustomed to the distractingly painful noise, he focused on Ebra. Something inside Evander told him to step into the dimming light in order to get closer to Ebra. Rowan's soul was almost completely inside the syringe when Evander threw himself at Ebra. They fell with a loud thump to the floor, and Evander wrestled with Ebra for the syringe now filled with Rowan's soul.

Ebra held Evander down. He had taken on the task of saving his community and friends, but now he realized the entire world was in jeopardy too. Ebra's hands were wrapped firmly around Evander's neck. He was choking and writhing violently on the floor, but he saw the syringe, dropped and forgotten, just a few feet away from where Ebra had him pinned. He reached his arm out as far as possible, grabbed the syringe, and jabbed the needle through his pants and into his own thigh.

Evander's vision became skewed. Ebra seemed bigger, and the walls seemed closer. He felt his body contract every couple of seconds, and his heart had almost ceased to beat completely. Ebra was yelling at him, but he heard nothing. No ringing, or his own voice, or a choir singing hallelujah as he reached spiritual consciousness. His eyes rolled back in his head.

Ebra stood up and ran down the hall toward the master bedroom.

Suddenly, the world was normal again. From one moment to the next, it felt like nothing had ever happened. He remembered everything except Ebra leaving. He stood up slowly, careful not to make himself dizzy, and made for Willow's door.

With the help of Rowan's soul, he was able to harbor enough energy to dematerialize, walk through the door, and appear inside the room where they had been keeping Willow. She was passed out on the floor. It was a dark room, not much different than the dining room, but Evander wasted no time taking in details. He ran to Willow and shook her awake. She mumbled incoherently, and he hoped he had gotten to her in time.

"Willow. Can you hear me?"

She scrunched her eyebrows and murmured, "Evander?"

That was good enough for him to take her in his arms and transport them back to the physical realm.

Right then, Ebra swung open the bedroom door, saw his captors had disappeared, and screamed obscenities. He had failed as both captor and leader. He dropped the gun he'd retrieved from the master bedroom, fell to his knees, and screamed even louder, scaring Eira who was outside the door, sweeping Rowan's ashes into a dustpan.

***

Evander and Willow were in the safety of Zan's backyard. It was a dark and starry night, which made Evander question just *how much* time had passed since they were abducted. He held Willow's limp body steady in his arms. Evander felt concerned about Willow's lack of strength. What she was going through was in no way healthy for a young girl with a young soul.

Zan burst through his back door. He had felt Evander and Willow's energies in close proximity. He ran towards them, nervous and excited. "Where's Rowan?" he asked, looking around his backyard, thinking she landed elsewhere.

Evander looked up at him and shook his head. "She didn't make it." He paused to take a breath. "And we're doing great, thanks for asking."

It was nine o'clock at night. Willow woke up enough to stagger inside and curl up on Zan's sofa with a thick blanket and some tea, while he and Evander talked privately in the kitchen. Zan stirred spoonfuls of honey into his tea while he listened to Evander ramble on about what he and Willow had endured.

Evander rubbed his forehead. "I can feel her. Like she's swimming inside me. What would make her do this? For someone who worshipped the earth and goodness, it must've taken something heavy to cause her to go to the dark side. And that girl, Mirele...I never saw her after I got thrown into the basement. She's probably dead. I think it was her soul I saw Ebra inject into his arm. Unless she was part of the plan, too, and I'm the fool." He shook his head, ashamed that his heroism was fading and he was becoming more and more a victim.

"I tried everything to find you," Zan said, putting his mug down to free his hands. "My bedroom is a mess from the spell-work aftermath. It was like you were dead, and I mean *really* dead. Willow too. I thought they had killed you both. Whatever power they possess, it's bigger than we thought. They're playing God, and that can't end well."

***

Zan drove Willow home before the clock struck ten. She couldn't conjure up the willpower to speak after the day's events. When Evander was taken out of the dining room in hell's mansion, the guards came back for her and Mirele and forced them into their bedrooms. She never saw Mirele after that and hoped she was okay. Willow's parents were already asleep when she got home.

She crawled into her own bed. All night long, nightmares plagued her. Cardinals swarmed by the hundreds. The vibrancy of their red feathers stood out against the moonless, smoke-filled grey sky. Then all at once, they dropped to the ground. Their lifeless bodies decayed at an exceptionally quick speed, and the once-beautiful birds became sad piles of bones. She looked down at her arm and watched her flesh slide off, piece by piece. It happened all over her body, her skin peeled and burned, leaving nothing but her skeleton.

She extracted herself from the dream and forced herself awake. The digital clock on her nightstand read 4:11. Willow, as worn out as she was, was unable to fall back to sleep. She stared up, slightly delirious, still thinking about her dream and what it could mean. Since meeting Evander, she had slept peacefully, untroubled by the visions and images that used to haunt her nights. But they were slowly returning: the nightmares, the fear, and the discomfort. She felt as if her life was returning to its normal state with a side of potential sudden death. She no longer felt special to be part of something big; she felt scared.

She sat up in her bed and turned on the small lamp on her nightstand where she often left jewelry and reminders written on a colorful note block. The light from the lamp softly illuminated her mother's ruby ring resting on a round piece of cork, which was normally used as a coaster. She played with the ring now in the palm of her hand and examined the small scratches in the stone, as she always did when she was tired or nervous. She put it on and twirled it around then got an idea to try traveling through time on her own because she needed something to do with herself since she was unable to sleep.

Sitting cross-legged on the floor, in the silence and privacy of her own pale-yellow-walled bedroom, she focused her mind and energy on the ring. She channeled happiness and hoped for the best. Suddenly, she found herself standing in a crowded part of a big city. A concert had let out. She spotted her youthful parents with ease.

***

Ebra was a frantic mess, pacing from room to room, pushing pillows off beds and kicking the antique walls. His voice was hoarse from yelling. He threw fine china against walls and completely shattered a mirror with his fist, bloodying his knuckles.

He was enraged that a few *kids* with ego problems were savvy enough to slip out of his fingers. Not only did they get away, but they also *stole* a soul from him, a good soul at that. A soul he would've consumed. A soul he would've savored.

Rowan was a developed Idio, and he was looking forward to joining with her and her energy. She was so callow. He'd made her believe he had spared her life so she could join him to bring on Armageddon and she would be his queen. She was no challenge. Ebra couldn't believe his plans were foiled so easily. As much as he should've blamed himself for underestimating Evander, he threw all the blame on Eira.

Eira sat on a dining chair, watching Ebra's tantrum unfold. She loved when he was fuming with anger. His rage was alluring. She knew where she belonged when he broke chairs and tore curtains apart. She belonged with him and his desires and his love of control. Even if he refused to share his power with her, she knew, at the end of it all, she'd be sitting on a golden throne next to him. They'd witness the end of the world as everyone knew it. The last remaining humans would have to profess their dedication and devotion to their new lord, Ebra, or else they'd be destroyed along with everyone else. Or Ebra would use them as slaves.

"Those meddling weasels will be the death of me. If you don't take care of them, then I will, and I promise it won't be a pretty sight." Ebra clenched his jaw and growled through his teeth, not even earning a flinch or hint of surprise from Eira.

She looked him up and down, and then rose from her seat. Eira placed both her hands on the sides of Ebra's face, caressing him with the affection she knew he hated. "They won't do any more harm. I will take care of them, not to worry." Eira spoke with a calmness that got Ebra to stop seething.

He tore from Eira's embrace. "I'll be in my study." He stomped up the stairs and slammed shut the door to his study behind him. The goal never was for Evander, Zan, or Willow to catch on to Ebra's antics. Eira wanted to use Evander as bait, to lure Willow closer, so it would be easier to strike her. After Willow was taken care of, Eira would hand Evander over to Ebra, as well. After feeding Evander to Ebra, she'd enjoy capturing Zan. She looked forward to seeing the look in his eyes when she told him that the love of his life was gone forever.

She had learned from her mistakes and was ready to do whatever she had to in order get rid of the three problems at hand. She would do it for no one other than Ebra. Her first target would be Willow. She was young, unsociable, and full of angst. Most importantly, she was available and seemingly easy, but not easy enough, all thanks to a young man who believed he owed her his protection. That belief would cost him his life.

***

"What about...a scythe?" Zan asked Evander. It was very early in the morning or very late at night, depending on how he looked it at, and they were buried in books. Almost every book was pulled from Zan's shelf: books about ancient gods, mythology, religion, and witchcraft. They were looking for anything to explain why Ebra was devouring souls. Then they could find a way to demolish him and his plans. In their research, they found no trace of any similar event that happened in the past. They reached a lot of dead ends.

Evander raised his eyebrows, questioning Zan's silly idea. "You want to kill Ebra with a scythe? Like the grim reaper? That kind of scythe?"

Zan shrugged. "It'll work, right? We find a scythe and chop his head off, like Keith Jennings in The Omen."

"Do you take this seriously, any of it?"

"Of course I do. I'm just saying, why not?"

Evander rolled his eyes. "You're a child."

Neither of them slept, so they drank coffee on

Zan's porch. They watched the sun rise and tried to count how many leaves fell from the trees. The sky turned from grey, to pink, to pale blue in a matter of minutes. The world was changing, and it will continue to change. New advances would be made in technology, polar bears might become extinct, and natural disasters would continue to occur. The world grew just as much as anyone, and when it died, its memory would live on with those souls who had the privilege to learn and live on the earth as they knew it.

"One of us has to get close enough to Ebra in order to off him." Evander made cutting notions with his fingers across this neck.

Zan took a sip of his coffee. "Are you implying that you're the one who wants to do that? Or is there an option?"

"I'd take it upon myself, sure. Do you have a problem with that?"

"I don't think any of us should sacrifice ourselves. I have a problem with this in general. Maybe fleeing the country isn't such a bad idea."

"Ebra's got our scent. He's like an attack dog. Running won't fix the problem here. He's still gaining power. He's still killing innocent spirits who deserve to live long lives. Ebra has an ulterior motive, we can't forget that."

Zan nodded.

They didn't bring up the subject again and decided they'd talk about it at a later time. When it came time to part ways for the day, Evander went back to his apartment and Zan prepared to go to work. Willow made it back from the year 1995 unscathed, and woke up lying on her bedroom floor with an empty stomach and a bad taste in her mouth. On her way downstairs, she heard her mother talking to someone on the phone. Most of what she said sounded mumbled.

As soon as the talking ended, Willow walked down the last couple steps and marched into the kitchen, simply nodding to her mother who sat solemnly at the table a few feet away.

She scowled at Willow. "I haven't seen you in a while. It's like you've dug yourself into a hole."

Willow poured herself a cup of coffee. "Who was on the phone?" she asked, moving past the subject of her detachment.

"Another psychiatrist, since Dr. Everly didn't work out for either of us."

"I don't need to see a doctor," Willow said. "I am perfectly healthy. In tip-top shape, even. I'm just a little worn out. A little overwhelmed. All that is normal. I'm not a fish out of water. I'm a fish in a pond, but I belong in an ocean. There's a difference." She took a sip from her coffee. "It's all about perspective, Mom. It's all about looking at things in a different light. Everybody goes through periods of growth, right?"

She nodded.

"I'm...*shedding*."

Then came an awkward silence. Elizabeth squinted, tilted her head, pursed her lips, and took several deep breaths before gathering the strength to respond. "I think you've said more words to me in the past few minutes than you have in months."

Willow gulped and focused on the warmth of the mug in her clammy hands.

"I don't know what to think about you anymore."

Willow rolled her eyes in a bratty fashion and tried to sound convincing. "Don't think. Let's have lunch. You can talk to Evander and Zan. Maybe they can convince you that I'm fine. Whatever Dr. Everly told you about me, forget about it. She's a leech. You can't trust her just because she has a doctorate degree. She could have all the degrees on a thermostat and it still doesn't mean she knows anything."

"You sound like your father."

Willow chugged the rest of her coffee and placed her mug on the counter. "We're gonna have lunch." She felt sorry for her mother. What Willow had experienced when she went back in time to see her parents' love unfold was inspiring yet tragically depressing. Their eyes were doting, full of tenderness and romance. Their hearts were still warm and inviting. Somewhere down the line, they grew apart and closed themselves off. Their promises to be partners for life through sorrow and happiness became buried deep in arguments and mixed feelings. That was another reason why Willow was bitter about love; there was no guarantee that it would last forever, which of course was debatable. Could anyone really fall *out* of love, or was that an excuse people used to justify separation? Love shouldn't have boundaries. Love should last for centuries. But just because it should, didn't mean it would.

Concepts often got lost in translation.

Even though Willow was the girl with the *No Regrets* tattoo on her forehead, she knew she wouldn't do well under the pressure *love* would put on her. Ebra's plans for genocide she could handle. Finding out how life and the universe worked was also something she could handle. Love? She was fine with leaving that for Evander and Zan to figure out, because her parents and millions of other people sure couldn't.

Willow was busy trying to keep her anxiety under control. She shot Evander a quick message. *Meet me and my mother at Clara's diner.* He didn't question her request and agreed to meet them. She knew she was acting out of character, but she hoped her mother wouldn't notice.

***

Clara's was crowded with bad-tempered men and enthusiastic teenagers on their lunch break. Willow heard no bells ring when she walked through the front door. She was thankful for that. The host seated Willow and her mother far back at a corner table. She was thankful for that too. When Evander walked in, Willow waved him over. Elizabeth gazed at her, brows furrowed, as if she wondered about Willow's joy to see him.

Wearing a black hooded sweater and dark jeans, he made a beeline for their table. His face showed signs of exhaustion; it seemed he had been awake all night.

"Mrs. Ferring." Evander held eye contact with her as they shook hands. "It's very nice to see you again."

Elizabeth nodded and smiled in response, though she seemed wary of how genuine he acted.

As soon as he slid into the seat next to Willow,

he asked if they would mind joining hands for a prayer. They obliged. He recited a short phrase in Latin so quietly that he could barely be heard.

"Quaeso imploro. Ego pro pace supplicemus. Ego pro amore. Ego pro viribus. Benedictus."

Willow knew why he asked, too. He was scared Ebra was coming after them, which was a very valid worry. It was dangerous for them to be out in public. After reciting his incantation, Evander kept the conversation flowing. He occasionally looked at Willow for prolonged periods of time. They conversed about domestic topics like the upcoming winter and family recipes for the holidays. After their food was served, Elizabeth loosened up to Evander, even smiling and laughing at his theatrical way of telling stories. Willow excused herself to the restroom, knowing her friend and mother would make it a point to talk about her behind her back.

"Is there anything I should know about my darling daughter that I don't already know?" Mrs. Ferring asked, resting her chin on her folded hands.

Evander flashed a smile. "Do I give the impression that I know more about her than you do? I think you're fully aware that Willow is a lovely person. She undermines herself, but she is very smart and intuitive. Characteristics she inherited from you, perhaps?"

"I just want her to be safe. I want her to have a future."

Evander reached over and laid his hand on Mrs. Ferring's. "Her future is bright and her future is promising. Everyone must grow and learn in order to progress."

Mrs. Ferring giggled. "Funny. She said almost the same thing to me this morning."

"See? We're all on the same page then."

When Willow came back to the table, Evander was staring intently at her mother, and her mother was looking down at the table shyly. It was like they had shared a secret. But Evander had actually worked a bit of magic on Willow's mother. Of course, power had limits. Evander, nor anyone, could take control of someone's mind completely. However, living for centuries had given him plenty of time to find loopholes and learn new tricks. She could call it reverse psychology, but whichever, Evander was capable of accessing Elizabeth's weaknesses just by focusing on her energy. He would never do that on Willow or Zan. Zan would catch on to him right away, and he would feel guilty for taking advantage of Willow.

Willow's mother, however...getting inside her

head wouldn't hurt anyone. She would feel eased about Willow's whereabouts and feel confident as a parent. Evander hoped whatever he did would benefit Willow somehow. He knew she had problems within herself, like feeling the need to conform to everyone's ideas of perfection and normalcy but not wanting to. He felt that any weight he could lift from Willow's shoulders would help her sleep a little better at night.

***

Ebra stalked the Art District of downtown Rosaphene. A necklace with a topaz charm hung around his neck. His dark eyes pierced through each person who crossed his path. Some stared back, some turned away quickly, and some even scowled, but all were clueless as to how puissant he was. In all his existence, he wanted the upper hand. He wanted the control of the puny human souls wandering aimlessly on the earth.

He was close. He could feel it stirring inside him, the energy built stronger with every soul he took. Ebra closed his eyes and basked in the moment. He pulled open the door to Crossroads and approached the counter with confidence and a menacing smirk. He was just about to tap the little silver ring-for-help bell when Zan popped out from the back room.

Zan stopped dead in his tracks and widened his eyes at the sight of Ebra standing in his café, hands in his pockets and devilishly good looking as ever. Zan composed himself and strode to the cash register. He kept eye contact with Ebra and said nothing. He was not prepared to cause a commotion in front of dozens of people with access to cell phones, and he couldn't risk the cops showing up, as if that was what he should've been most concerned about.

"Won't you be so kind to whip up a nice warm cup of hot cocoa? It's getting a bit chilly." Ebra spoke slowly and mimicked shivering.

Zan leaned forward and whispered through his teeth. "It'd be best if you left, *sir*." He expected Ebra to snap his fingers and transport him to some kind of purgatory, but he just stared as if Zan was his lunch.

"I will leave," Ebra stated. "But this is not a goodbye. I will find you, I will find your damsel, and I will find your prince." He looked around and returned his gaze to Zan. "You cannot stay safe from me for long. The clock is ticking, boy. You better get to burying some of those skeletons in your closet before it's too late, yes?" Ebra spun around and strolled out without even looking back.

Zan breathed in, then he breathed out, wondering if what had happened was real. They had received an official, stamped, and addressed threat. Ebra was a certified sadist, finding pleasure in slow torture and instilling fear in his victims. Zan wiped a few drops of sweat from his forehead and looked up at the ceiling. He hoped it wouldn't be the last time he would see that ceiling. He hoped it wouldn't be the last time he'd overhear conversations about ex-boyfriends, rude grocery store clerks, or why dogs deserved eternal life. He hoped it wouldn't be the last time he had to wear an apron *in public*. He hoped there was a hopeful future.

However, Ebra wasn't joking. Zan and his friends were not ready for what he expected to come...nothingness. What he saw next, through his anguish after his interaction with Ebra, was Clarence staring at him from across the room.

Chapter 8
TIME

The death of a soul was no laughing matter. Zan was terrified to his core to find out what it felt like to not exist, if it would feel like anything at all. He had been alive and sentient for a very long time. He watched millions of sunrises and sunsets, he watched history being made, and he had lived to tell every tale. With the death of his true being—his true self—would come the death of his memories and past. Death didn't seem so scary or intimidating after going through the process every once in a while. Every time his body died, within seconds he would extract himself from the physical realm and become conscious in the form of another anthropoid. What happened between life and death was quick and void of feeling anything whatsoever. Reincarnation was a walk in the park, and it became like any other trivial daily activity. He figured a higher power always took care of him.

But where was that higher power? He felt angry and flushed that the deity in control of the world was nowhere to be found. He thought that while the planet and everyone on it were being burned to ash, the deity, or god, or *something* would come down from above on fluffy white wings to save the day. He was not averse to stereotyping what God might look like. The big guy, or girl, wore a jewel-encrusted crown and a velvet cape. God didn't wear faux fur, though. That would be too tacky.

Zan placed his palms down on the counter to support himself. He felt faint and shaky. His vision was clouded with dark spots and blurry shapes. He heard customers come in, so he forced himself to an upright position. He couldn't focus enough to see their faces, but he knew they were female, and they were already ordering before he could ask how they were doing. Zan wasn't stable enough to work, but as long as the world still spun, he had a job to do and strong coffee to brew.

After he took the new customers' orders, he saw Clarence walk toward the counter. His hair was slicked back with gel, and his t-shirt was wrinkled. "Is everything okay?" Clarence asked with a look of concern, a rolled-up newspaper in his hand.

Zan nodded, tears beginning to well up in his eyes. He wasn't in the mood for anyone's sympathy. "Fine. Just fine."

Clarence nodded back at him and excited the coffee shop, looking back at Zan one more time before disappearing into the daylight.

***

Evander was slumped over his bathroom sink. He had a massive headache and a fever. When he returned to his apartment after his lunch with Willow, he felt like he had gotten in a fight with a brick wall and lost. He was lightheaded, gasping for air, and he had thrown up. He splashed water on his face and looked in the mirror. His eyes were bloodshot and they burned so bad that he couldn't keep them open for long. Evander had suffered plenty of headaches, but this pressure he felt was indescribable.

The pain, the vomiting, the dizziness: they were all symptoms of his body accepting Rowan's soul. Her soul was aware of what was happening, and soon, her consciousness would diminish and her energy would completely merge with Evander's. He was going through the same symptoms that Ebra went through every time he injected a soul into himself. Ebra was more experienced, and he had gained enough strength to combat the sickness.

Evander dragged his feet all the way to his bedroom and tossed himself onto his bed. He didn't care how he landed or in what position, he just needed to sleep through the struggle.

That night, he dreamt of Rowan. He dreamt of her in the form he had last known her. Her lustrous red hair shone bright in the sun of a hot summer's afternoon. Her eyes glistened with the forgiveness and kindness Evander knew she had in her since the beginning of her existence. She reached out to touch him, and he swore he could feel the gentleness of her fingertips on his jaw. In his dream, he closed his eyes to treasure what turned out to be the last time he would ever see her.

When he opened his eyes again, the image of her faded way, and he was left standing in a field alone. The sun beat down on him, and the wind made a whistling noise that transfixed him. He reached out to midair and wished Rowan would reappear in front of him. He wished he could tell her that he forgave her, but something told him that she already knew he did.

Willow had an interesting dream of her own.

She was sitting on a cement floor, surrounded by four cement walls. It was another dream that involved a bird. She was alone in the room, except for a very large cage holding a small canary. She watched the bird bounce and fly inside the cage. Its wings fluttered in panic. Its feathers fell off, and its bright yellow color turned white. It became weaker and weaker by the second and eventually dropped to the bottom of the cage. Willow frantically looked for an opening or door to the cage; she wanted to help the poor thing, but she couldn't find a way in. She brought her shaking hands up to the steel bars and held tightly onto them with what little strength she had left. She felt the cage wobble. The bird transformed before her very eyes...into Zan. His body took the same position as the bird, lying on his side, one arm slung over his head. She became even more frantic, calling out his name over and over. She shook the cage as hard as she could.

Zan's eyes twitched and shot open. He immediately found Willow and stared at her so intently it seemed as if he was staring through her. He gradually sat up straight to face her, and over her own hands, he grabbed onto the bars and leaned his forehead against them.

"We are but pawns in this eternally

maddening show," he whispered.

She woke up.

***

The next morning felt very strange for everyone who resided in Rosaphene. Willow felt the need to hide. She didn't care to step foot out of her bedroom, as if the room was some sort of protected safe zone. Evander started to feel less like someone who was dying a slow death from his migraines. Neither of them had heard anything from or about Zan. He seemed to be missing in action. Evander tried calling him several times and was sent to voicemail. He sent Willow a text, asking her if she had gotten a hold of him. She then tried to contact him, too, but had no success.

Willow was on the phone with Evander. She rubbed her forehead, stressed. "I want to know where he is as much as you do, but I don't think it's best to go out right now."

"Ebra can get you if he wanted to, and you know that," Evander stated matter-of-factly. "Your house isn't protected. You'd be safer with me. I'll be waiting for you at Crossroads."

Before Willow could argue about meeting up with him, he hung up on her. She got dressed as fast as she could and rushed out of her house without looking back. She walked briskly down the sidewalk, her head down and arms crossed over her chest. She breathed in through her nose and out through her mouth, trying not to exude fear.

On the way to Crossroad's, she ignored many greetings from strangers. She ignored how beautiful and bright the leaves looked on some of the trees. She ignored the way the sky looked. She ignored her surroundings in favor of her goal, to get to the café alive. She felt as if she was being watched, perhaps by the birds flying overhead, or by the children who felt the need to stare. Someone or something was keeping a very close eye on her and the rest of Rosaphene's population.

When she stepped inside Crossroad's, Willow found Evander right away. He was sitting on one of the sofas, reading the newspaper. He seemed calm and collected.

"Did you know Clarence Novak opened a bookstore on Seventh Street? There's a story about it in the paper." He pressed his index finger against his lips, as if he were silencing himself.

Willow plopped down next to him. "Why is that important? Have you heard from Zan?"

"I've always wanted to visit the Grand Canyon. We should go on a road trip."

"Excuse me?"

"What do you say we pick up a dozen donuts and head back to my place? I bought that powder to make strawberry milk. Do you think strawberry milk would taste good with donuts?"

Willow blinked a few times. Evander hadn't been acting strange over the phone. "What's gotten into you?"

He groaned. "I'm so tired, Willow. I'm so tired. Everyone's gone missing, or dying, going crazy, or crying...and it's too much." He slammed the newspaper into his lap and let his head hang. "Am I even alive right now?"

"Well," she began, "are you breathing?"

"Yes."

"Is your heart beating?"

"From what I can tell, yes."

"Are you capable of thinking?"

"Maybe too much." He stood up from the sofa without explanation and walked straight out of Crossroad's.

Willow followed him. She worried he would do something stupid, and she had to be there to stop him if he tried.

Before she knew it, she was sitting in the passenger seat of his car. He drove slowly to his apartment, turning every corner with caution. She never took her eyes off him. He could snap at any moment. She had never been so afraid.

Thankfully, he didn't snap, and they arrived at his apartment safely. As they climbed the stairs to his floor, they both felt the need to look over their shoulder every couple of seconds. Evander unlocked his front door with unstable hands. When Willow crossed through the doorway, he slammed the door shut and locked it. He strode into his kitchen and prepared a teakettle.

"Did you see the stars last night?" He took out two mugs from one of his cabinets.

"No." Willow hadn't made time to stargaze since meeting Evander. She hadn't made time to do anything since meeting Evander. Things were different. She was different. The entire *world* was different.

"They were bright. They reminded me of Zan. They reminded me of you."

Willow was at a loss for words, worried she might say the wrong thing and set him off. As he did his thing in the kitchen, he mumbled to himself, something about donuts, from what she could understand. She wondered why he was so fixated on donuts. For a short moment, she considered getting some donuts for him. She wanted to do anything to help him. She took a moment to really look at him. He was wearing a navy button-down shirt and dark jeans, a silver ring, and some stringy bracelets. His hair was, as usual, messy and curly, but his face looked expressively softer.

"Starting a new lifetime is weird," he said as the kettle started to sing. "You have to adapt all over again. You have to go through adolescence again, you have to learn to drive again, and you have to grow old again. In the back of your head, you know who you really are, and you're aware of your past lives. But it's not until you're at least a teenager that you start to grasp the concept of reincarnation. It's a slow reveal and it feels very awkward, but once the realization happens, a lot of things start to make sense."

Willow took a few steps closer to Evander while he poured hot water into the mugs. "You're worried about Zan, aren't you?" She placed a hand on his shoulder.

He relaxed at Willow's touch. "Extremely. I've lost him once already, and I can't lose him again. It would tear me apart. I would be broken."

"Zan was in my dream last night. Do you think it could've meant something?"

Evander spun around to face Willow. He searched her face frantically before meeting her eyes with his own. "What was he doing? Did he say anything?"

"He called us pawns. Something about being pawns. Something about...a show?"

"I'm gonna kill him. Unless Ebra gets to him first, let it be known that I will be the one who ends his life once and for all."

Willow managed to smile at Evander's remark. "He's fine, Evander. Can't you feel it? He's fine."

Evander nodded and gulped. She knew he knew deep down that Zan was okay. As strange as the day felt, she knew for a fact that nothing bad had happened to him.

The morning sunlight beamed through Evander's windows. As time passed, Evander loosened up for the sake of staying somewhat sane and told Willow stories from his past lives. She enjoyed listening to him talk and found his insight of the past fascinating. He told stories of times she had always wished she could've lived through. She was able to de-stress under the spell of Evander's cinematic voice and dictation.

The earth was a strange place, and time was a strange concept.

Willow didn't feel as if her life conformed to that concept anymore. It didn't seem all that important to count minutes, or days, or years.

Living meant more than numbers. She remembered Evander telling her something during her first visit to his apartment, about how he would show her *a better perspective*. She thought, while watching the expressions on Evander's face change as he told his stories, that she had finally seen that better perspective.

You are not living until you forget that you're living and accept your existence, you accept the inevitable, and you stop putting off a trip to see the Grand Canyon because waiting will take you nowhere. Time doesn't start or stop for any mistakes, for any changes, or for anyone.

She could tell a lot about people by how they handled tragedy and misfortune. Evander might have been breathing steadily, but inside, he was wailing. He couldn't understand how one man found a loophole in the rules set at the beginning of creation. Evander was frightened to think that Ebra spent his entire existence working for a chance to become an almighty and powerful crazed overlord who would bring about detriment and death. Was it destiny that Ebra would be the reason why modern-day souls ceased to exist? Maybe in the books, the true books unknown to mankind, scribed by the original source of life, it was written that a man of terror would reign and cause mass hysteria as souls met their inevitable deaths. Evander considered that Ebra, perhaps, wasn't capturing souls and leading them to their deaths, but maybe Ebra *was* death itself.

The thought made Evander sick. He didn't want to tell Willow, though he felt the end was near. Regardless of how twisted his view on the world was or how fear was eating him from the inside out, an end of *something* was inevitable. Since he became aware of the murders as they occurred, Evander walked the world on his tiptoes, and yet he still had the nerve to drag Willow into the disaster. Of course, if she had stayed unaware of the truth, she might have been an easier person to target...and therefore be dead already. He figured that if she knew who she was, the secrets of the world and the danger that being alive posed, then her chance of surviving might be higher. But as it turned out, knowing more wasn't always better.

Then something hit hard against the window, startling Willow and Evander out of their musings.

Evander jumped up to look, and on the outside of the window, he saw a black crow. Eira had been sent as a warning. Everyone knew that a crow was a bad omen associated with darkness and death.

Evander should've realized that Eira had been used as a decoy for what was to come, all along. As his eyes met those of the woman he'd grown close to since one of his first few re-births, he felt like an unforgivable fool.

When the bird squawked at him, he hit the window, scaring Eira into flying away. He turned toward Willow, face flushed and jaw clenched.

Willow had already felt tricked by a white rabbit before, but she felt that way even more so now. Except, she no longer saw Evander as the rabbit.

"We should just launch ourselves into the dark depths of outer space," Evander murmured and fell to the floor where he curled into a fetal position. Swimming among the stars, finding a new home on a distant planet, exploring previously undiscovered galaxies, and screaming where no one could hear him: they all sounded like amazing things to do. An even more amazing thing would be to live on earth without having to look over his shoulder in fear that someone would steal his soul and use it as fuel to incite the end of the world.

Willow felt appreciative of humanity. It was hard to fathom that her time as an earthling could be cut short.

***

Ebra planned to strike, but he was too distracted, too caught up in drama, and he had to get his mind straight. On the edge of a cliff, near Rosaphene's largest cemetery, he stood watching over the small town that would soon be destroyed. It would be the first town he would wipe out, and it would be an accomplishment worth celebrating. He planned on taking Eira somewhere nice, where the weather was always warm, where they could spend a few days of relaxation before going back to work. Eira deserved to feel pampered, since there would come a time he'd be forced to make a decision about her demise.

The days of devilry were approaching, as dusk fell earlier and days became shorter. At night, there was more opportunity for wicked activities and mischief. There was little time left for his young *friends*. Every clock in Rosaphene was set to stop in unison, every soul worthy of injection would become a part of him, everyone else would be burned, and their energy would be stored for future plans. Ebra couldn't be greedy, taking every soul as his own, not leaving any for use down the line. After all, he had no idea if his powers would eventually wear off and he'd have to revitalize. The souls he'd keep locked away were merely in case of an emergency. He had a special hammer ready to break the jars constraining their purple auras.

The next town he wanted to tackle wouldn't be a town at all. Ebra wanted to attack something bigger. Something better. A place with more variety. A place with more color and culture. He considered New York City, Los Angeles, or Rio De Janeiro to experiment with different ways to burn a multitude of bodies and capture all worthy souls. His lighter was a good enough weapon, a lighter filled with the energy of Hephaestus. He'd owned that lighter for a very long time, but he had been waiting for a moment or sign to use the powers within it to his advantage.

That time had arrived at full speed, like a train on a track that stopped in Rosaphene.

***

Zan kept himself busy and isolated. He tore his home apart, casting spell after spell, reading incantation after incantation, praying on his knees for what he promised himself would be the last time he ever willingly prayed. There was no religion, there was no recovery, and there was no safety.

Fuming, he transported himself to *Centrum Labyrinth* and screamed at the top of his lungs. The serene room was quiet. He disturbed the peace by grabbing every record book on the first floor and throwing them violently at the ground. Peace was a figment of everyone's imagination to help everyone continue living without wanting to jump off a bridge every five minutes. *Peace is not real, peace is not real,* he said to himself as he tore pages out of the books, though the pages grew back, reappearing as if he hadn't torn them out in the first place. Still, he felt relief. His anger had been building up for a very long while, and it was about time that he released some of that rage. He didn't want to hurt his friends. He didn't want to scare anyone. He had to go where no one would hear him curse the day the universe was created.

"Is this what you wanted?" he yelled at the taunting velvet door. "Was all of this part of your divine plan?"

The distant sound of a clock ticking distracted Zan from his tantrum. It was coming from a few floors above him. He walked to the staircase and began to climb it. As the clock sounded closer, he wondered if it was always there, and if he just hadn't noticed it when he first entered the labyrinth.

Torches lit up his path, and a thick carpet of a color his eyes couldn't process silenced his heavy footsteps. Looking at the carpet made him feel sickly, so he kept his attention straight in front of him.

After climbing the stairs a few floors, he could tell exactly which door the ticking was behind. It was a black one, and it invited him to turn the knob. He swallowed hard and considered transporting back to his house, back to his friends, and back to face his reality, a world beset by evil. Something nudged him forward, like a gust of wind; it pushed him into opening the door. For a second, he thought he heard someone call his name, but he couldn't be sure. What he faced now was far scarier than a ghostly voice calling out for him.

Behind the door was Eira's office, and behind Eira's desk sat Eira, one spindly leg crossed over the other and her eyes set on Zan. He looked around and noticed that it wasn't like her office exactly. In this replica there were no windows, no connection to the outside world. He was still in the labyrinth, just in a different room. Because of that fact alone, he felt safe enough to approach Eira's desk, though cautiously.

"You don't look well. Maybe you should take a

seat," she muttered.

"I wanna know what all of *this* is." He swept a finger around the mock office.

"This is nothing more than what you think it is. I think you should be focusing more on why *I'm* here."

"Okay, I'll bite. Why *are* you here?"

"Because I knew you were coming." She leaned forward, her eyes emptier and deader than before. "And I have something very important to tell you."

Zan stood quiet, waiting for Eira to continue speaking.

She stood up and glided to him with confidence. Eira was mere inches away from Zan, and yet he still felt that she wasn't a threat. Even when she pushed a few strands of his hair away from his face with her cold hands, he didn't budge.

"Would you do anything in the name of love?"

Zan pondered the question, then, "No. Not anything. I wouldn't kill for love, unlike yourself."

"Darling, I believe you have the wrong idea of me. I am not a killer. I am not here to bring you harm, but you already knew that, didn't you?" Eira smirked.

Zan nodded, staring at her dry lips, noticing

the lack of wrinkles on her face despite her age. "What do you want from me?"

"I want nothing from you. But I *would* like to give you something. This will surely help." She reached into the pocket of her suit skirt and pulled out a black bag barely big enough to be a coin purse. It was tied shut with a thin red ribbon.

Zan took the bag from Eira's fingers and inspected it closely, fearing to open it. When he looked up again, she was gone. He looked around the room, wondered where she had disappeared to. The little black bag was warm, but strange enough, whatever was in it gave off very cold vibes. Vibes that made Zan want to throw the bag and its contents into the deepest ocean, hoping it would never be touched again.

He turned around and exited the replica of Eira's office. As he walked back down the staircase, he felt that whatever was in the bag was thin, hard, and oddly shaped. There were only two things he thought about doing with the bag. He went with his first idea. He would open the bag alone, in the safety of *Centrum Labyrinth*, as opposed to opening it with his friends—who didn't know where he was or what he was doing—in the ever-so-dangerous physical realm.

Zan stopped in front of the mysterious maroon

velvet door. He looked it up and down, ran his hand along the soft textured material with the same interest that Willow had shown when she first came face-to-face with its magnificence. It was beautiful and intimidating in a way that doors to the unknown could be. It had an attitude too. A mocking sort of attitude. It stared Zan down as much as Zan stared *it* down, as if the door was alive. Zan looked at the bag in his hands and untied the thin red string. In the bag was a key, a bronze, slightly tarnished key that felt dangerous to hold. He looked from the key to the door, back to the key, and back to the door.

The key.

The door.

So much...and so little made sense. The silence in the room grew thicker as his nerve grew stronger. Again, he had to make a difficult decision.

Attempt to open the Velvet Door with the strange key given to him by one of the most untrustworthy beings, or transport back to his friends, and make a decision about the key together.

Only a few seconds passed before he made up his mind. In denial about how unsure he really was, he stuck the key into the lock and gave it a twist.

***

Evander moped around his apartment, grieving his own coming death. Willow watched as he washed dishes that were already clean, and she listened as he mumbled pessimistic remarks. Hours passed and he gained some solace. Willow stared at him and rolled her eyes a handful of times. She was losing interest in feeling sorry for herself. There was no point in sulking about something that hadn't happened yet. Evander was bringing her down.

Willow, tired for no specific reason, was ready to tell Evander she'd be leaving to go on with her day, and that he should be doing the same. As she gathered herself, Evander's eyes widened at something behind her. She spun around and came face to face with Zan, whose eyes were wide and excited. Before she could say anything, Zan rushed to Evander. As Evander regained his balance, after being shaken by Zan's sudden appearance, Zan touched his arm, and they were gone from sight.

Still uncomfortable with the thought of effortless transporting and time-traveling, Willow threw her hands up in acceptance. Whatever made

Zan tear Evander away in the manner he did, especially after dropping off the grid, was none of her business. Besides, she needed space to think. She needed to isolate herself for the sake of self-preservation. Whenever Evander or Zan requested her presence, she'd be more than willing to oblige.

***

Zan needed to speak with Evander privately. He transported him to a place that had once been significant in their past lives together, a place that only existed in their thoughts and memories.

Evander looked around as he stood in place. "Why did you bring me here?"

The house looked exactly the same, as it should. "It was the first place I thought of when I touched you." Zan gulped. He had something very important to discuss with Evander, but it seemed that Evander had thoughts and opinions of his own that he needed to voice. Zan gave him the time. It wasn't like the Velvet Door and the secrets behind it were going to run away. Or at least, Zan hoped that it wouldn't run away. That would've been unfortunate for everyone involved.

"Are we not going to continue dancing around the fire, adding fuel to the flame? Is this your way of addressing our issues?" Evander asked with a joyless tone.

"I've already chosen to stay. What more is there to address? I've sensed no friction between us."

"There's been no friction. Just neutrality. You know how I hate neutrality."

Zan shook his head. "You can't possibly expect anything more. The walls have been broken down."

Evander squinted at Zan, who was clearly missing his point. "You are so unbelievably stubborn. You're tiresome, infuriating, and immature."

"Keep going. I'll stand here and listen to you all day, if that's what you want."

Evander continued without delay. "And I have yet to forgive myself for what I did to you back in 1968. Had I realized the magnitude of what we had, I never would have pushed you away. But the past is the past, right? We're expected to grow and rebuild what was torn down many years ago. Do you expect me to somehow fix what I broke by bringing me to the home we shared when you loved me?" Evander was on the verge of tears. He had almost perfected the art of bottling up emotions.

"When I loved you? I *do* love you. But that isn't

why we're here. I would be more than happy to continue this discussion, but I think you'd be far more interested in what is currently in my pocket."

Evander quickly rubbed away the wetness from his eyes. "What's in your damn pocket?"

Zan immediately pulled the old bronze key and dangled it in front of Evander's face.

He looked mostly confused and offended by what Zan showed him. *What's so special about a key? If this is his way of being funny, I'm not laughing.*

Zan smiled. "Use your imagination. If you could open any door, any door in the world, which door would you open?"

In unison they said, "The Velvet Door."

Evander stopped breathing at the exact moment he figured out that Zan's key was none other than the key to the Velvet Door. The door he, and many others, had tried to unlock, break down, and force open. How Zan had acquired the key was a question he needed answered.

"I'll explain later," Zan said. "But you won't believe the things I've seen. From what you've told me about Ebra's *process*, I think the souls he doesn't inject, he hoards. If Eira is on our side or not, if this is a trap or not, taking a few of those souls is worth a try. If we can gain enough power to measure up to Ebra's, we could have a shot at a fair fight."

Evander felt betrayed knowing that Zan chose to open the door on his own, without consulting anyone about it first. But if he was being honest with himself, he knew that he would've done the same thing if he'd had the chance.

"We shouldn't bring Willow into this," Evander stated. "Not yet. Tonight, we should unlock the door together and you can fill me in on what you know."

Zan nodded his agreement. "Every time I forget about how bossy you are, you find a way to remind me."

Evander took a deep breath. "Zan, I am so terribly sorry for everything I've—"

Without even having the chance to finish the apologetic monologue he had written out in his head, Evander was mostly forgiven. Zan sealed his forgiveness with a kiss that seemed far too sentimental, considering they should've been unlocking the velvet door, stopping Ebra in his tracks, and saving the human race. *But how much fun is the end of the world if it isn't romanticized?*

While lying in bed alone, tossing and turning, Zan was mostly overwhelmed by thoughts of Evander and how he wanted to approach their relationship...at least, what was left of it. He considered keeping Evander at a distance. Forgiving Evander didn't mean he'd have to keep him near and dear. But as ostentatious and emotionally inept as Evander was, Zan still decided that Evander made his existence better. With their past in mind and not forgotten, they prepared for what they thought would be a very short-lived future. Zan knew that Evander's often erratic actions would never be justified, and he found his peace in knowing that.

***

Zan met up with Evander later that evening at Rosaphene Park, near the same spot Evander and Willow once spent time stargazing. It was a quiet night, except for the revelry of some intoxicated people circled around a fire pit. Evander leaned his back against a tree as Zan stood staring at the bright white moon hanging ominously high up in the sky. They were procrastinating. Zan was nervous about returning back to The Labyrinth with Evander, not because he feared Evander would go into a panic or throw a tantrum, but because he had a feeling someone unpleasant would be waiting for them. When Zan first opened the Velvet Door, his sense of logic was attacked and defeated. He hoped Evander would have a better idea of what to do with what was behind the door, and whether they could use any of it to save themselves and everyone else.

"Before we go," Evander said, relaxed under unusual circumstances. "What's the story behind the key?"

Zan looked down at Evander and heaved a sigh of trepidation. "Would you believe it if I told you Eira willingly handed it to me?"

Evander moved his head from side to side, as if attempting to crack his stiff neck. "This could be their way of allowing us to think we're one step ahead of them."

"Why would they do that?"

"They're sadistic. This might as well be a televised game show."

"If that's the case, is going through the Velvet Door in an attempt to fight back even worth it if this is all one big game to them?"

He sprang up and palmed Zan's cheek. "You *never* stop fighting. No matter what. Let's get a move on, shall we?"

Zan laughed. "You and your strange English, *get a move on*. What century do you think this is?"

After responding with a lighthearted smile and wink, he transported himself and Zan to The

Labyrinth, ready to make some exciting and slightly nerve-racking discoveries. The Labyrinth was unusually warm. Zan headed straight for the door and held the key near the lock. He looked back at Evander, and Evander gave him a nod, telling him to go ahead and open the door. Zan took a deep breath and unlocked the lock then pulled the door wide open, which revealed nothing but pitch blackness behind it. He moved to the side to let Evander further examine the mystery.

Evander, with a knot the size of a meteor in his throat, reached into the nothingness and stroked the darkness cautiously, as if he was shaking hands with a stranger.

"You have to step forward," Zan said lowly, his entire body shaking from the suspense of watching Evander make friends with the darkness. In order to see what was in it, the room had to trust him. Earlier, he had gone through the same process, the process of stepping into the unknown, the unlit unknown, trusting the shadows and allowing the shadows to become aware of every one of his intentions and feelings.

Evander heard them whispering, the Undergods, the acolytes of the first and truest Deity. But he couldn't determine whether the whispers were pleas for help to save them or encouragements to join them. There were so many whispers, each word tangled with another. Sentences tied together, expressions that couldn't be deciphered.

He was uncertain about stepping forward. "Something seems very off about this," he said, hoping Zan felt the same way.

"Step forward. I came out alive, didn't I?" Zan wanted Evander to get on with it.

Evander got flashbacks from when he found Rowan in the basement of Ebra's mansion. It was a sense of déjà vu, like he had found himself in the same trap. He hadn't felt uneasy about anything toward Zan before, or at least not in the same way or for the same reasons.

"Did you come out alive?" Evander asked. "Did you really?" Suddenly, he did not recognize Zan's face, now unable to see who was wearing the mask of his life-long love. Evander was losing his touch.

Zan smirked in a way that looked distorted and alien.

"Eira." Evander breathed out, and he was forcefully pushed into the darkness by hands that were not Zan's.

What both Evander and Zan didn't see up

above their heads at Rosaphene Park, hidden behind thick branches and the last crunchy leaves left that hadn't yet fallen to the ground, was a black crow perched in the tree Evander had leaned against. She had tailed them all day, from the moment Zan took the key from her, up to the point Evander attempted to transport himself and Zan to The Labyrinth. She was sent to follow them in a desperate attempt to end two out of three of Ebra's problems.

As Evander dematerialized, the crow attacked Zan, causing him to flail and tear away from Evander's touch. Zan tried to shoo the bird away, but she reached in his pocket and snatch the key, and then disappear with it. He was left on his own, still in the park, piecing together what had happened.

Zan was tired of being left to figure everything out on his own.

***

The last face Evander saw was Zan's morphing into Eira's. He was swallowed whole and digested by the darkness. His screams produced no sound, they just made his throat feel like it was being clawed at. He ran in circles, reaching no walls or end. His body trembled, he fell to the floor with his hands planted firmly on the ground; his arms were too weak to hold up his body. He involuntarily closed his eyes, meeting the familiar blackness he saw when he fell asleep at night, but now he was distracted by the phosphenes. He was knocked out for no longer than a few seconds.

When he came to, he was no longer surrounded by the darkness that originally consumed him. He was lying on the floor, a bit of saliva seeping from his lips, his cheek pressed to the cold hardwood. He picked himself up. His eyes did not appreciate the spotlight shining directly at him. He made an effort to shield his face from the scintillating light. Was he a character in his final act, showcased to an audience of one?

He walked forward, looking down at his feet as they moved closer to what looked like the edge of a stage. There, he saw rows upon rows of empty theater seats adorned in the same maroon velvet as the Velvet Door. He turned around and was face to face with a thick curtain made of the same material, hanging from ceiling to floor. He stroked it, confused, scared, and more powerless than he had ever felt. After following the curtain to one end, he moved enough of it to the side for him to step behind it.

Behind the curtain was not an area for actors to

change outfits or rehearse lines before appearing on stage. Instead, he found himself in a vast stockroom with an endless number of shelves that were at least a few humans tall. There was no light except for the vividly glowing purple orbs trapped in spherical glass jars. He picked up a jar and held it tightly in his hands, knowing exactly what that purple light inside was: a soul. A soul which had been extracted from a body burned to ash and now trapped in something as simple and deplorable as a glass jar.

He remembered what it was like to see Rowan turn to flames. Her energy was still inside of him, from when he managed to steal Ebra's syringe and injected her soul into his bloodstream. She swam inside of him for hours, his body wanting to reject her like it would an organ transplant. He missed how Rowan always smelled like fresh-picked flowers and nail polish remover. He missed driving around town with her during late hours when they were both restless; they'd explore abandoned buildings and sneak into cemeteries. Rowan was a free-spirit, never bound to rules or regulations. She would always be the girl who carelessly danced in the middle of her living room at five in the morning, wearing a fancy dress and worn out heels she'd bought at a thrift shop. She'd spent most of her money on art supplies and hair dye. She was there for him after his initial breakup with Zan. He cried for hours, weeping in regret and sadness. She did whatever she could to console him.

Rowan's last lifetime was Evander's favorite, but he wished she would've had the opportunity to live longer. He wished they'd all have the opportunity to live through more, especially after a glimpse of what it was like to be *with* Zan again, something Evander once thought never would've been possible.

He felt a sense of impending doom as he held a wrongfully imprisoned soul in his hands.

"You can't deny that this chase has been rather fun," Ebra said, hovering somewhere close by.

"You might need to reevaluate your idea of *fun*," Evander said, not at all in the mood to bounce sarcastic comments back and forth with Ebra.

Ebra cackled like an old witch. "Did your darling bury those skeletons of his? Don't worry. Eira is taking good care of him and the *girl*."

Steam could've blown out of Evander's ears. His body temperature rose to the degree of the sun. His grip on the glass jar tightened as Ebra's laugh bounced off the walls of Evander's skull. In one swift motion, he threw the jar to the floor, expecting it to break in a million tiny pieces. But it stayed intact, not even a scratch.

Ebra raised an eyebrow at Evander, who was panting and whimpering like an injured animal. He had nowhere to run. Nowhere to hide. He was alone, face to face with the enemy, ready to lose what he thought was his final battle. With Zan's cordiality and Willow's intrepidity on his mind, he didn't feel as if he would go down in ignominy.

***

Willow walked home after Zan stole Evander away. It was a longer walk than she was used to, but she had no problem with that. The closer she got to her house, the slower she walked, the worse she felt. There was a complete shift in the world, as if the ground was tilting and the sky was cracking and about to collapse. She felt feverish, and absolute terror boiled in her stomach. There weren't many moments she had ever felt that way, but it was like anticipating the drop of a rollercoaster. She was nearing the edge, in sight of how far down she would crash.

She walked up to the front door of the home she never felt safe or happy to live in. Staring at the door, she knew it was unlocked, but she was apprehensive about opening it. Tears streamed down her flushed cheeks. With an unsteady hand, she reached out and grabbed the doorknob, using all of her strength to turn it and open the door that would never get the new coat of paint it needed.

Before stepping inside, she looked around her front yard. For some reason, she knew then, that would be the last time she would ever find herself apprehensive about stepping inside that house. She knew that was the last time she would ever look down at her shoes, buying time, not wanting to call that house *home*. For that, she felt guilty, because that house was where she had lived out important years of her life, and she wished she had better memories of her time here.

As she walked inside, the tears subsided and her body stopped shaking. The first thing she noticed was how all the curtains had been closed and all the lights were turned off. The house seemed to be in the same shape she had left it in when she met Evander at Crossroads. She listened for any unusual sounds and looked around for any objects that might be missing or purposely misplaced.

Sweeping. The sound of sweeping and whistling came from the kitchen or the dining room. She headed toward the sound with a feeling of regret and grief. Her breathing was shallow, and her heart was fast, beating like it wanted to escape from her ribcage. The distance from the front door to the kitchen felt like miles, even though it was really only a few yards. Her feet dragged across the floor.

I shouldn't have left home this morning. She was closer to the sweeping sound; she turned a corner and found her father, dressed in a wrinkled button-down shirt. He was holding a broom and sweeping up a pile of ash.

"What are you doing?" Willow asked, her voice high pitched and sharp.

Her father said nothing at first. He momentarily stopped sweeping and looked at his daughter without even a shred of emotion.

"Dad?"

Her father blinked in annoyance and sighed heavily. "You're late. I'm afraid you've missed pizza for dinner." He continued sweeping.

Willow stepped backwards. The man in front of her looked like her father, but she knew her father was not inside that body. He would never eat pizza or allow her mother to bring pizza home for dinner. Willow didn't want to find out who was really standing in front of her.

"Let's have a chat."

"No." Willow shook her head. "This is wrong."

He tilted his head to the side. His back was straight and shoulders square. He leaned the broom against the counter and walked toward Willow while slowly sliding a hand in his pant-pocket. Willow kept backing away, knowing that if he were to get closer, something bad would most definitely happen to her. She observed the way he walked with poise and sophistication, very unlike the way her father walked.

"What do you want?"

He pulled a gold lighter out of his pocket and held it firmly between his thumb and forefinger. Willow didn't recognize it, but Evander had seen it up close and personal on the day Ebra incinerated Rowan. Evander had described the gold lighter to Willow. She clenched her fists and took a deep breath before bolting for the front door.

He tossed the lighter at Willow and laughed chillingly, missing her by a few inches just as she ran outside. The flame caught onto the curtains, spread wild and quick, and eventually engulfed the entire house in fire.

Willow ran as far as her feet could take her. She was breathless and terrified. Evander was gone. Zan was gone. She was alone and more susceptible to harm than ever.

She ran from her house all the way back to Evander's apartment and curled up in front of his purple door. It wasn't the most hidden place she could've found, but she had nowhere else to go. Her house was burning down and she could hear the fire trucks zooming down her street. Her parents...she didn't even want to think about what Ebra had done to her parents. She didn't want to think about what must've become of them while she was gone. Whatever happened to them, they didn't deserve it, and Willow felt sick again.

Remembering who she was, Willow weakly stood up and closed her eyes, amassing the energy she had left to defy the laws of physics and walk through Evander's door. Being inside the apartment seemed much safer than sitting outside. When she opened her eyes, she was standing in Evander's apartment. She collapsed to the floor and sobbed until she had no more tears left. Her heart was crushed.

The sun had set but she saw no reason to get up and turn on the lights. She wanted to be alone in the dark and wait for the entire world to explode and burn. Dying, she would see visions of sugar plum fairies, take her last few breaths, and wait for the end to happen.

She must've waited long enough because she heard heavy footsteps in hallway outside, and they stopped directly in front of Evander's door. Death had arrived. The doorknob jiggled frantically. She closed her eyes and braced for the appearance of Ebra or his henchwoman, Eira.

The door opened abruptly. Heavy breathing mixed with panicked moans caused Willow to open her eyes and turn around to face her killer. Lights flickered on, and in her view stood Zan. He looked like a complete mess, drenched in sweat and in distress. They stared at each other, both lost as to what one another were doing there.

Zan shut the door and locked it, as if that would protect them from the terrors of the outside world.

"Your house," Zan said, his voice scratchy and worn from screaming. "It burned down."

"I know," Willow muttered.

After Eira attacked him at the park, he went to find Willow in fear that she was the next target on Eira's hit list. Zan was afraid to lose both people who meant the most to him. Evander was smart, tactful, and usually quick on his feet. Zan knew Evander wouldn't go down without a fight. He was holding on to hope, having found it deep within himself by some miracle.

Seeing what was left of Willow's house made Zan lose his mind. All he could think about was the possibility that she was trapped inside while it burned down; he would never forgive himself for letting her out of his sight, if that had been true. Thankfully, that hadn't been the case. They both felt as if they had dodged a bullet.

"They've seized Evander."

Willow lifted up her head. "Where is he?"

"The Labyrinth, I think. He could be elsewhere, but knowing what's behind the Velvet Door, rescuing him will be perilous."

"We're going to die tonight, Zan."

He shrugged. "The chance of that happening in the next few hours is high." The way Zan spoke reminded her of Evander. After their reunion, they became more connected with each other than ever.

Willow nodded and stood up, tall and with honor. "Transport us to The Labyrinth then."

When you don't have much, you can't lose much. Willow understood that clearly. She didn't know what her life would be like if she survived the night. Everything would be different, obviously, considering her parents seemed to be gone from the life she knew, and her house was history. She had no money, no extended family, and no inflexible aspirations.

But there were still the stars. The stars were forever. *When one door closes, another one opens. When one world ends, another one starts.* There was an end to everything, but there was always a beginning, too. Willow wouldn't leave her world scared, or sad, or full of hate. She would go in a neutral state of mind, knowing that the price to life is death: unavoidable, inarguable, death...without resurrection or reincarnation to back her up. But she felt that, even though her time on earth was short, she had succeeded. She did not fail herself, and for once, she was confident in her life and in her existence.

***

Zan transported himself and Willow to The Labyrinth. It was dark, like the light in the core of the world had been turned off. The curtains were ready to close, and the actors were ready to take their final bows. The Velvet Door was still open, waiting to entrap the last two flies in its web. There was no going back. There was no more pride or shame. Willow walked toward the door, where she heard whispers. The same whispers Evander felt disconcerted by before he was pushed into the darkness. She listened carefully, trying to listen for words of warning or persuasion. Lucky for her, the real Zan was with her to keep her from running in too soon.

"The darkness is friendly, but it took some getting used to. I've gone in before so I should go first and check things out before you follow me."

Willow shook her head, ready to argue for her right to lead them into battle. "I'm going in with you."

He was in no mood to fight with her. Zan just nodded and took her hand in his.

"Relax," was all he said and walked with her past the Velvet Door and into the darkness.

***

Evander shifted into his animal form, a slick black cat with piercing blue eyes, a bald spot behind his right ear, and a missing tooth. He'd gotten into some trouble a while back and never fully recovered from the boot-to-the-face damages he endured.

Ebra rolled his eyes as Evander scampered away. He was about to reach the heavy velvet curtain when Ebra popped up in front of him, causing him to trip over his own paws. But Evander slid between Ebra's legs and rounded the curtain, sliding back onto the stage where the spotlight still shone. However, the stage was not empty.

Two figures stood in the light, hand-in-hand. Zan and Willow. *Guess we're all a bit sacrificial.*

Evander hurried to them, still in feline-form. Zan spun around when he heard Evander's thoughts in his own head. He blinked, and Evander had shifted back into his human form but stumbled during the switch from paws to human feet.

"It's about damn time you came to save me," Evander joked breathlessly, putting his hands on his hips and smiling as though he wasn't about to be attacked.

The heavy velvet curtain swayed. Ebra popped out from behind it. The light reflected off of his clenched teeth and sharp cheekbones. He lifted a fist in the air and swung his arm as hard as he could. A shiny gold object flew through the air toward them. Zan hadn't quite made out the shape of what was about to hit them until he saw a flame, and his brain went into emergency-mode. He pushed Willow and Evander to the ground and covered their bodies with his.

The lighter crash-landed on the floor, unlit. Ebra sprinted toward it while yelling threats and promises to finish what he started. Promises to be victorious.

Zan wouldn't have it. He got up just fast enough to slide across the floor to the lighter and grab it before Ebra leaped toward him.

Zan heard his name screamed out, followed by pleas to stop, but he didn't allow himself to give into Ebra's nefariousness.

Ebra picked Zan up off the floor and shook him like a rag doll, but he refused to let go of the lighter. The next thing he knew, he was being pummeled, causing him to fall into a daze, but he did not let go of the lighter.

He was thrown to the ground.

Two strong hands cut off his breathing.

He saw stars.

Zan took one last breath.

Suddenly, memories from his past lives flooded his mind, which brought him a sense of peace and calmness. He saw Evander. He felt Evander's hands caress his face. Evander's words told him everything would be okay. Zan remembered that day. The year in which that memory originally took place escaped him, but everything else was clear as day. They had been sitting on a park bench for quite a while on a warm summer day, talking and feeding hungry pigeons. Children played loudly, couples were on dates, and older folks were happily walking their dogs.

Zan had been feeling down about himself for no distinct reason. At one point during their lengthy conversation about what it meant to feel nothing and everything at once, Evander had turned to him and held his face in both hands. He breathed out and kissed the top of Zan's nose, making Zan blush and forget about his intrusive worries for just a few seconds.

"When you're unsure everything will be okay, know that I'll always make sure everything *will be okay*." Evander had said it with a small smile.

Zan bowed his head at that remark and nodded, trying to believe the one person he felt believed in him.

Zan closed his eyes, letting his memory with Evander absorb him. He loosened his grip on the lighter, and Ebra snatched it. Then the tightness that was around his neck disappeared and he gasped for air. His vision came back slowly as his memories faded.

Evander yelled at Willow to stay on the floor, and he launched himself at Ebra. Ebra rose up and flicked Evander off of him like a bug, because to Ebra, Evander *was* just a bug. He stared down at Evander, who was scowling, staring up at the ceiling. The spotlight was now on Ebra, the true star of the show.

"I get it now," Evander whispered. "I see the light."

At that remark, Ebra furrowed his bushy eyebrows. The many shades of silver in his hair gleamed. The three scars on his temple were no longer there, as if the energy he injected into his body repaired him to great lengths. All of those repairs were about to be undone, because a fool was a fool, and goodwill always outweighed evil.

Eira suddenly came skidding in on her stilettos with *Butch* in her arms. No one saw where she came from. Evander picked himself up and kicked the back of Ebra's knee. As Ebra collapsed, it gave Evander the chance to confiscate the lighter, set the wick aflame, and throw it at Eira. The last words to escape her thin lips were the beginnings of an apology, an apology that would never have the chance to be voiced nor accepted.

The flames that engulfed Eira were rather unremarkable and much smaller than Rowan's. She screamed as her body, along with Lorelei, aka Butch, burned to ash. The room fell silent and everyone stilled. Ebra watched them die with a frown on his face.

Evander and Willow watched from their places on the floor. Willow knew that her parents had met their demise in a similar manner. Evander gulped, remembering that he still held Rowan's energy inside him.

"How unfortunate," Ebra said as Eira's and Lorelei's souls floated into the air, dim shades of purple, barely bright.

Evander turned to Ebra, not in disbelief that no one seemed to care about Eira's ashes or her drifting soul. He held eye contact with Ebra, and they watched each other closely. *Don't be afraid.* Evander breathed deeply, not knowing if he was telling that to himself or to Ebra, and he prepared to duck or block a punch.

Ebra moved closer to Evander and stared. "What great games these have been," Ebra boasted, as if thinking he had already won.

Evander shook his head. "What *is* your motive, Ebra? I can't understand why you'd want to rule a world with no one in it."

"Last Man Standing is the best role to play."

"That sounds like a lonely life."

Ebra shrugged child-like and smirked. "Loneliness is a figment of one's imagination."

"You know what's quite sad?"

Ebra bobbed his head. "You?"

Evander laughed and looked at Willow, who had crawled across the room to retrieve the lighter from near Eira's ashes. With the force of her entire being, she threw the lighter, praying it would hit Ebra. Though it flew in the right direction, nothing would've caught Ebra *that far* off guard.

Evander's glance had given Willow's position away, and that was a huge mistake, because Ebra's awareness of the lighter allowed him to hold his hand up and catch it effortlessly between his fingers.

That was the moment everyone thought their lives were over. The moment that would dictate how their legacies would conclude. The moment that Ebra would rise from The Labyrinth and take the crown of the world.

Ebra laughed deeply and winked at Evander before lighting him on fire. Evander heard Willow shriek and Zan scream his name as the fire quickly caught onto his body.

There was something about being on fire that was really liberating. It was a strange sensation, but Evander did not feel fear. He did not feel compelled to scream when he caught on fire like Eira did just a few minutes earlier. Evander felt peaceful and content. A lot of that had to do with the fact that Rowan's smooth voice echoed in his head, which overpowered the high pitched ringing. Evander smiled at the sound of Rowan's words. "Attack before it's too late."

Just before his body turned to ash and the flames ceased growing any further, he lunged forward and latched himself onto Ebra.

The spotlight flickered off. The only light that kept the theater from going pitch dark was the fire moving from Evander's body to Ebra's. The flames engulfed him. He screamed, angry because he failed, and angry because he would get no chance to destroy the world. As the fire turned colors, Evander's soul rose above it into the air. Ebra's soul did not, as he didn't even have one, but every soul that he injected himself with did rise up, one by one, reclaiming the dignity that had been taken from them. They all floated in midair, swarming each other in celebration of their freedom. They looked like bees, if bees were purple and glowed brightly like neon signs.

If Zan hadn't known any better, he would've said that he was absolutely terrified when Evander's soul grew brighter, bigger, and stronger. The entire theater filled with the intense violet light of countless souls. The experience petrified him. One might think that an explosion of energy meant *the end*, but Zan knew better. Instead of seeing *the end* when Evander's soul burst like a balloon, he saw the beginning. They were all sucked into a tunnel, into an otherworldly tube that was about to spit them out when it reached where they needed to go. In a flash, Evander and Zan both saw all of their past lives. All of their memories, the good and the not so good, replayed at lightning speed. Memories they hardly remembered came flooding back with clarity. Willow saw only the memories from the life she had been living, since it was only her first one. She hadn't realized before then how long she had been living, what effort it had taken to survive each year.

They were experiencing the truest and purest form of nirvana; and it was beautiful. The other side was too beautiful for words, too beautiful for mundane descriptions. There were not enough ways in any human or alien language to explain what it was like to break the barriers of time and mortality.

Chapter 9
REVELATIONS

"**A**ll the things said about the number *three*, you know, that it's magic and all, that's true. I think you should know that," a familiar male voice said in the darkness.

Willow knew she wasn't breathing, but by some miracle she was still conscious. "Are we dead?" she asked, feeling silly about it afterwards.

The man speaking harrumphed. "I had a feeling you would ask that."

Someone snapped their fingers, and suddenly Evander, Zan, and Willow were able to see each other, looking quite like themselves as they were before. They stood on a mountain under a massively large tree, unlike any tree they'd ever seen before. Carved into the tree was the shape of a door, with a golden doorknob sticking out, unmistakably. Looking around, they took notice of the endless fields of flowers and grass, the countless trees, rivers, and animals roaming freely. The sun shined down, warm and inviting. It welcomed them happily with its bright beams of luminosity, like a spotlight would, showcasing the performers, giving them their moment to take their bows. Giving them their moment to feel proud of their craft, of the lives they portrayed and acted out.

"Hello there," the man said, finally showing himself to them. "We've all met before but I feel like I must formally introduce myself."

Willow dropped her jaw, not believing who stood tall in front of her. "Clarence?"

The man who bore a resemblance to Clarence Novak of coffee shop fame smiled. "Sure. You can continue to call me Clarence. After all, I am who you want me to be." He looked at Evander, "How do you feel? That was some suntan, huh?"

Evander was at a loss for words. "Confused, mostly. How is it that I'm still alive?"

"Oh, certainly you are not."

"Where are we?"

Clarence looked up and around. "You know where you are. In fact, you all know where you are. What you don't know is why you're here and how you got here. As much as I'd like to give you all the answers and details, I won't. Not because *I work in mysterious ways* or whatever, but because it's not your time to know just yet...unless I want it to be time."

Zan raised his hand as if asking a teacher for permission to speak.

Mr. Novak pointed at him. "Yes, Zander?"

"Did you know what Ebra was doing?"

Clarence nodded. "Of course. I know everything." He clasped his hands behind his back. He was there the entire time. Willow, Evander, and Zan never noticed. They were all too caught up in the disturbances.

"Why didn't you do anything to stop it?"

"Me?"

"For that matter, why don't you do anything to stop everything that's wrong with earth? Because you have to know, there are a lot of things wrong with the world *you* created." Evander's voice was laced with annoyance and a tone of disgruntlement.

Willow felt embarrassed by the attitude he was giving Clarence.

Clarence sighed and thought carefully about the best way to answer the question that had been on Evander's mind for a while. "I'm asked that question very often, as you might imagine. As much as I'd like to be truthful, I think that would ruin the idea of *choice*. Don't you agree that if *everyone* knew how much or how little control they have over their own lives and the future, that the magic of living would be lost?"

Evander nodded, knowing no other answer would be given, but he was not pleased.

Clarence stared at him for a short while and sighed again, but more heavily. He let his head hang and dug the heels of his oxfords into the rich green grass. Clarence hadn't always been so in-tune with emotions, but over time, he wanted to feel more connected to the humans, to the lost souls that prayed for forgiveness, love, health, or money. Willow's father wasn't too far off when he preached about the stars hearing every wish that was wished upon them, only the stars weren't the ones that were listening. It was always Clarence.

"I know what you're thinking." Clarence shifted his focus to Zan, who was just about to ask another question. "Every soul that Ebra captured and tortured will be given a choice. As will all of you, though your choice is much different."

He paused to scan the dumbstruck faces around him. "This is an unusual circumstance. Balance has been lost. Some sort of control needs to be regained. If I don't at least *try* to follow my own rules, this universe would be much more reckless than it already is. I allow humans far too much freedom. My sympathy toward people can get in the way at times."

Clarence took a deep breath. "But it would also be against my morals to not make an exception for the three of you. You did whatever you could to protect your own kind, each other, and your loved ones. There are not many souls as bright as yours. My job is not easy, and I have to admit, I do get lazy sometimes. But I must not have slacked off when I created you."

Zan scoffed. "Then why did you put us through all this?"

"I didn't. You did, of your own free will." Clarence cracked his knuckles and spent a few seconds staring off into the distance. "But since I'm sure your wish is to be resurrected, to be tossed back into the salad-bowl we call earth, to continue living and being reincarnated as if these past few wretchedly exhausting events never happened, then so be it. Consider that you will be completely restored, so therefore, you will remember everything that has transpired."

"If we don't want that..." Evander squinted skeptically. "What's our other choice?"

Clarence signaled to the abundant gardens around them. "Isn't it obvious? Your soul lives on here. You'll experience true peace. Tranquility. This would be the ultimate spiritual voyage, as it was originally designed. Those are all the details I am at liberty to give out about this place, but if you decided to stay here, there's no going back. There is no returning to the physical world."

Zan huffed. "Sounds boring."

Clarence smiled at that remark and shook his head. "It's great that you're judging something you don't know a thing about. Seems like your screws are finally loosening up."

He was nothing like anyone thought he would be, the almighty celestial being who they only knew as Clarence Novak. The same *person* who dressed in drag on any given day and wore Billy Idol shirts was the head of Mission Control upstairs. He proved the myths surrounding him to be true. Well, at least some of the myths. Willow was happy with who was watching over them, though. Knowing that the one and only deity collected weird belt-buckles and mocked certain politicians helped her regain optimism.

"I don't want to encourage you to lean towards one option more so than the other, but there is a lot of work to be done on earth. I have paragons of virtue to assist me here, but they're not fleshy beings such as yourselves." Clarence sounded much more serious than before. "Many spirits will be reborn. Many spirits will be newly born. Because of Ebra, we lost quite a few of our guides. We will eventually fix what's been broken. I can't put my trust in those I feel will not be of help, but I will put my trust in you three, because you've proven yourselves to be renegades in favor of the greater good. That's what matters."

Willow crossed her arms and stepped forward, looking intently at Clarence. "If we choose the former option, will we ever see you again? *This* you, in particular."

"I'm touched." Clarence set a hand over his heart. "Yes. I will continue to always be with you. In fact, I am *everywhere* with *everyone* always. How's that for a riddle?"

The three *renegades* thought about their options. Without saying anything to each other, they were keen on making a decision as a group. They had gone far together, and it would be a shame for them to separate at this point in their existences.

Clarence zoned out and looked around Eden, rocking back and forth with his hands in the pockets of his jeans.

Willow watched him with the same intrigue she always had when she watched him. She listened to him whistle and take everything in stride, assuming he already knew what decision they were going to make in regard to their futures. Zan and Evander stared at each other, discussing the best road to take without using any words. Evander glanced at Willow, and she nodded her response back at him. The big light in the sky kept shining as if it hadn't stopped since the dawn of time.

Evander cleared his throat. "We all agree with you on the notion that the earth would suffer terribly without us on it." His joked earned a laugh from Clarence. "We'd like to be resurrected."

Clarence nodded proudly and clapped his hands. He rubbed them together excitedly and turned toward the door that was carved into the tree behind him. Clarence turned the knob and opened the door. The inside of the door was covered in maroon velvet. "Consider yourselves part of a society only I and my Undergods belong to. We call ourselves the *Velvet Door Society*. You still hold the key that unlocks our door. Don't be afraid to use it again."

Clarence waved to the door that would allow them to exit Eden and return to their physical world. "You will be helped across and through

The Veil. Step in whenever you're ready."

Willow, Evander, and Zan held hands momentarily before they each stepped through one at a time. The last to leave the garden was Willow. She felt melancholy to leave such a heavenly place. She and Clarence shared a moment that she would only describe as reassuring. He raised his hand and placed it on the side of her head, subjecting her to a kind of simple affection that Willow had always been afraid of. She hadn't quite understood what love truly meant until that moment of clarity. Without love, the world would've fallen apart very quickly, shortly after it was created. It was a small gesture, what Clarence had done, but she would always be thankful to him for allowing her to have a second chance to accept what life was really about, for allowing her to learn to feel without fear.

"See you soon," Clarence said, dropping his hand and waiting for her to step through the door. She gave him one last glance, even though she knew that she *would* see him again. But she knew she wouldn't see him like she saw him in that moment, at least not for a very long time. She never expected she would feel so connected to such a divine energy.

Taking a deep breath, she stepped through the

door into the darkness, anxious but happy about leaving her past behind, to start a new adventure, hopefully a safer one.

***

They found themselves in The Labyrinth. The Velvet Door closed behind them. Whether Ebra had twisted their perception of what was behind the door, or whether the gate to Eden had been temporarily closed, didn't matter. The shelves of jarred souls were nowhere to be seen, probably set free for eternity.

Willow was in awe of what had happened to them, in awe of the one deity so many people worshipped, and in awe that the secrets entrusted to them would stay secret. What lay behind the door would never be revealed to another living being, for they also wouldn't want the magic of living to be lost, especially Looscents, Idios, and Numinists alike. They would leave The Labyrinth and transport back to the physical realm with their lips locked, their heads up high, and absolutely no idea what to do with themselves, considering only some order in the universe had been restored.

They grieved for the souls that were taken too soon. Evander knew that his relationship with Zan would never deteriorate. It had withstood the test of time. Zan wanted to get back to work at Crossroads, doing what he did best, serving customers and Clarence copious amounts of coffee. It would take a while for them to find their routines again, but they knew that, as long as they stuck together, nothing would be impossible.

As Evander transported them back to his apartment, Willow realized that she had no home. No family. No clue as to how to take care of herself in all human aspects. However, she wasn't worried about her future. Clarence had taught her that destiny would take care of her.

Evander wrapped her in a hug. "I promised I'd take care of you. I still plan on keeping that promise."

Zan laughed in a nervous kind of way. "Does that leave me to take care of *you*?"

Evander rubbed Willow's back and slowly tore himself from her and stood closer to Zan. "How about we just take care of each other?"

"Sounds right to me." Zan smirked and pulled Evander into a tight embrace.

Willow looked on like a parent, proud that her children were finally getting along.

Zan kissed the corner of Evander's eye, making Evander squirm from the sappiness of it all, of actually feeling stable for once, after having experienced the most unstable of happenings.

"Don't pretend you don't love it," Zan mocked Evander's visible discomfort.

Evander rolled his eyes and pulled away. "I love *you*." He felt powerful saying those three words again.

And Zan felt secure hearing them.

Willow had nightmares for a while following her return to normalcy, but she fought hard to rid herself of any negative thoughts. Eventually the feeling that someone or something was *still* watching her would dissipate, but until then, she was on guard. She went back and forth from both Evander's and Zan's places, sleeping wherever it was convenient. When she visited Zan while he was working at Crossroads, she sat at a table with Clarence. He would smile and nod at her, and she would smile back. They'd talk about little things, and she'd pick his brain like she loved doing before she found out who he really was. She felt like herself again, only more confident in who she was as a human, and she had more faith in everyone around her. Clarence was happy that she had taken control of her life.

***

A few weeks after what was supposed to be

the end of the world, Willow enrolled in the university to major in astrology, and she got a job at the planetarium. She worked for her own money, got her own apartment, and bought all new clothes to replace those she'd lost when her house burned down. Her parents were officially listed as *missing persons* and the insurance company wrote her a check for the loss of their home.

She woke up one Saturday morning and lay in bed, thinking about how her life had changed. However, one thing she knew remained the same. Time: *Time doesn't stop for any mistakes, for any changes, or for anyone.*

It was time to stop wasting time.

She proposed the idea of a vacation to Zan and Evander. Neither of them hesitated to agree with her. They chose to take a road-trip to the west coast to see as much country as they could and finally visit the Grand Canyon.

There is significance in everything we do, whether it's washing dishes or saving the human race. There is significance in greeting someone with a kiss on the cheek or a shake of a hand. There is meaning in how we perceive paintings and the music we listen to. And sometimes there's nothing wrong with putting oneself before others.

Willow, Evander, and Zan found significance in the Grand Canyon. Standing on the edge of nature's beautiful creation ignited a fire in all three of them. Because the earth was so much bigger than them, and the Grand Canyon was so much bigger than them, and the meaning of life was so much bigger than them, that didn't mean they couldn't be bigger than the persons they once were.

She felt more like a kid again than ever before, seeing magic in everything around her, being able to fall asleep to the sound of thunder again, and feeling like everything *meant* something. She knew that Evander and Zan felt the same way too.

Willow looked up to the sky and remembered that she was not watching the sky; the sky was watching her. She remembered being a young girl, running to the backyard to look through a telescope for the first time, and being astounded by the magic stars seemed to possess. The stars knew that no matter what decision she made at any given moment, she would end up exactly where she was meant to be.

About the Author

Shanaya Fastje is an eccentrically eloquent singer, songwriter, and promising young fiction writer, having penned four books by age twelve, graduated high school at thirteen, taken the national stage as a motivational speaker, and at fifteen, her self-help book "Bully in the Mirror" was voted worthy for Books to Movies by a panel of 126 judges. Shanaya's extraordinary achievements have been praised and awarded by many prominent figures including U.S. President Barack Obama. With a boundless imagination, Shanaya incites social justice by using fantasy-like narratives to evoke awareness of common tribulations. She continues to captivate us all.

ACKNOWLEDGEMENTS

I've come to the conclusion that, at some point in all of our lives, we say the words "I wish" – whether it's a wish to go back in time and do something differently or a wish for a material object. We walk a winding path of mishaps and adventures, and we call that path *life*. Along that path, we may be led through turmoil or distress, and we have to brush ourselves off in order to keep moving forward. However, we are also led through moments of happiness and bliss, absolute joy and cheerfulness.

Missions of mine have always been to tell stories, create meaningful art, bring about awareness of important issues, and make connections with people through something we all have in common: being human. I like to think that I have made strides with my work – such as with my music, writing, and public speaking – but I couldn't have accomplished anything, nor could I continue doing what I love to do, without the full support of both my parents. Here're my declarations of gratefulness and love, even though I've expressed my thanks many times in person (I mean, come on, we live together. I'm writing ten yards away from you).

To my mom (also known as: Mothership and/or Mama),

Whether we're listening to music in the car, sitting in an important meeting, discussing ideas for future projects, or looking for new restaurants to try, we find a way to make any situation funny and even embarrassing. You work tirelessly for me from dusk to dawn, and that in itself deserves an award and endless hugs. *One day*, you say, *it'll all pay off*; the hard work, the hours unslept, the tears shed in public bathrooms, and the laughs echoed through hallways of hotels all across America. (Remember that road trip, getting lost in the back roads of Virginia while it's pouring rain? Good times.)

We've moved from Texas to California, back to Texas, and then to Tennessee in the same red car, which has lost a few hubcaps along the way (that's fixed now). We've learned that opting to laugh at misfortunes instead of getting worked up over them is much healthier for our minds, and that not eating meat is much healthier for our bodies.

I love you, best friend – your adorable, curly haired self (even if you don't put enough cinnamon in the rice pudding).

To my dad (also known as: Daddio),

Half the time, I have no idea what city you're in, but that's because you're constantly on the move for work, and I can barely keep track of what day it is, let alone where you're working for the week. But the surprise packages that come in the mail, the products you've shopped for online from websites you're vague about, make me happy. What doesn't make me happy is when you have me look up bad disco bands from the 80's, which results in me having to listen to hours of songs that should be locked up securely in vaults on another planet (okay...it makes me a little happy).

Thank you for embracing my geekiness, my love for *Supernatural*, and for practically never letting me down. You work hard every single day and continuously make sacrifices, and that hard work shouldn't continue without being commended for it first (even though you'll argue that praises aren't necessary). For everything you do for me on a daily basis, and more, I love you. But I just wanna ask if you can pick up a hobby or something because you're way too hard to shop for (and no, watching shows about aliens isn't a hobby).

Okay, let's continue. Think of someone who has made a great impact on this world. Several people may pop up immediately, and one person may or may not stick out more than the others. That isn't to say that how we achieve greatness is some kind of competition. Everyone's passions and interests are different, so therefore, the people we think highly of differ.

When it comes to personal inspiration and motivation, the winding path I walk led me to a show called *Supernatural*, which led me to discover that someone named Misha Collins exists.

To Misha Collins (whom is the influence behind Clarence Novak, one of the coolest characters I've had the pleasure to create as of yet),

I like to call you a light, or more specifically, *my* light. I've looked up to you for some years now, and there is never a moment when I second-guess myself for considering you my hero. You've impacted my life, this world, and my perception of this world. There've been times when I've lost hope – in society, and in the future, even. There've been times when I've questioned choices I make – as have probably everyone who's ever lived – and questioned *myself*, what I think, and who I am. But somehow, you've restored a lot of my faith, and you've restored a lot of my bravery to wake up every morning with a *kick it in the you-know-what* - kind of attitude.

Because of you, my fight – for whatever I may have been fighting for – was stronger and indomitable. Because of you, I found the spark to finish this book – to push past the setbacks and ignore the nails scratching at the chalkboard – and to be confident in not only this book, but also in myself. You've shown me that we have to find fearlessness within *ourselves*, that we have to want to be better for *ourselves* first, and that at the end of the day, we have to be happy with *who we are*.

I'd like to add a thank you for celebrating differences, for your spirited *abnosomness* and willpower to make a difference, for helping me fully realize that other's opinions of me say more about them, and for not only standing behind the phrase *"you are not alone"* but also proving its truth. I catch myself thinking "What would Misha do?" quite often when I'm at a crossroad – the answer is always *keep going,* and *be kind to yourself so you can be happy enough to be kind to the world*.

Every time I've had the pleasure to be in the same room as you, I can't help but be taken back by the energy you exude. You never cease to surpass amazingness, and even though you may shake your head at that statement and think otherwise, know that it is true, regardless. I believe that you were created for a very special reason, and you have become tremendously important to me. Thank you for making it cool and acceptable to not conform to society's norms, to be compassionate, and to be proud of ourselves, no matter the reason. You've made my experience living on this planet much more special than it would've been if you hadn't been living on it too.

Shanaya Fastje

As the years go by, *Supernatural* becomes a bigger and bigger part of who I am. I draw inspiration from that show for everything I do. For those of you who don't know, in just a few words, *Supernatural* is about two brothers who hunt monsters, save the world a couple times, and fight for a greater good. However, *Supernatural* is more than a series about ghosts, demons, and angels. *Supernatural* is about family and rising above malevolence. It teaches that monsters are real, and they're out there, and sometimes they take human forms.

The *Supernatural* fandom is a *Supernatural family*, and without going into too much detail, this TV series, which has become more than just a TV series, has helped me create wonderful memories, most of which are of the conventions. So, here's to a show that is a huge part of why I love conventions, and also a huge part of how this book was written.

To Louden Swain (Rob Benedict, Billy Moran, Stephen Norton, & Michael Borja),

On nights when I thought there was no more of this book to write, that I reached a wall I couldn't possibly jump over, your music truly helped me *take a shot* and *plot my heart away*. On nights when I thought I couldn't possibly get any sleep because of racing thoughts and worries that would seem meaningless to other people, your music was there to keep me company. I have never emotionally connected with anyone's music as much as I connect with yours. I feel the passion and the love behind every song, and it's rare to come by music that is completely raw and honest. From my favorite songs, to the ones that make me cry (specifically *She Waits, Help You, Reunion* & *Downtown Letdown*), there is never a song that I skip. Most of this book was written to your music and most of my ideas sprung from listening to your music.

Thank you for being with me every time I sat alone at coffee shops, every time the room I was in felt too quiet, and every time I needed a boost of creativity. When my mom and I took a late night drive in November of 2015, I put *Help You* and *Downtown Letdown* in the car player and was singing along, tearing up, and I just *knew* that everything I feel (*ever*) is valid, and that there's no shame in simply *feeling*.

This world is filled with so much negativity and hate and disaster. But this world is also filled with a lot of love, resilience, and unity. There is a *light* at the end of every darkness. I wrote this book for those who need something to believe in, who need something to fight for, and who need something to resonate with.

Thank you.
I can't wait for tomorrow.

Velvet Door Society